SIMON & SCHUSTER CHILDRE

ADVANCE READER'S COPY

TITLE: The Broke Hearts

AUTHOR: Matt Mendez

IMPRINT: Caitlyn Dlouhy Books/
Atheneum Books for Young Readers

ON-SALE DATE: 09/19/2023

ISBN: 978-1-5344-0448-9

FORMAT: hardcover

PRICE: $19.99 US / $24.99 CAN

AGES: 14 up

PAGES: 240

Please send any review or mention of this book to
ChildrensPublicity@simonandschuster.com.

ALADDIN • ATHENEUM BOOKS FOR YOUNG READERS
BEACH LANE BOOKS • BEYOND WORDS • BOYNTON BOOKWORKS
CAITLYN DLOUHY BOOKS • DENENE MILLNER BOOKS
LIBROS PARA NIÑOS • LITTLE SIMON • MARGARET K. McELDERRY BOOKS
MTV BOOKS • PAULA WISEMAN BOOKS • SALAAM READS
SIMON & SCHUSTER BOOKS FOR YOUNG READERS
SIMON PULSE • SIMON SPOTLIGHT

THE BROKE HEARTS

ALSO BY MATT MENDEZ

BARELY MISSING EVERYTHING

THE BROKE HEARTS

MATT MENDEZ

NEW YORK LONDON TORONTO
SYDNEY NEW DELHI

A CAITLYN DLOUHY BOOK

An imprint of Simon & Schuster Children's Publishing Division · 1230 Avenue of the Americas, New York, New York 10020 · For information about special discounts for bulk purchases, please contact Simon & Schuster Special Sales at 1-866-506-1949 or business@simonandschuster.com. · The Simon & Schuster Speakers Bureau can bring authors to your live event. For more information or to book an event, contact the Simon & Schuster Speakers Bureau at 1-866-248-3049 or visit our website at www.simonspeakers.com. · The text for this book was set in ITC Kabel Std and ITC Galliard Std. · Manufactured in the United States of America · First Edition · 10 9 8 7 6 5 4 3 2 1 · Library of Congress Cataloging-in-Publication Data · Names: Mendez, Matt, author. · Title: The broke hearts / by Matt Mendez. · Description: First edition. | New York : Atheneum Books for Young Readers, [2023] | Audience: Ages 14 up. | Audience: Grades 10–12. | Summary: Mexican American teens, JD and Danny, still reeling from the gutting death of their best friend by police gunfire, grapple with life-changing decisions and the kind of people they want to be, for Juan. · Identifiers: LCCN 2022054090 (print) | LCCN 2022054091 (ebook) | ISBN 9781534404489 (hardcover) | ISBN 9781534404502 (ebook) · Subjects: CYAC: Grief—Fiction. | Best friends—Fiction. | Friendship—Fiction. | Mexican Americans—Fiction. · Classification: LCC PZ7.1.M4712 Br 2023 (print) | LCC PZ7.1.M4712 (ebook) | DDC [Fic]—dc23 · LC record available at https://lccn.loc.gov/2022054090 · LC ebook record available at https://lccn.loc.gov/2022054091

FOR
MARGIE
AND
GABBY,
WITH ALL
MY HEART

"You want to tell a story?

Grow a heart.

Grow two.

Now, with the second heart,

smash the first one into bits."

—Charles Yu,

How to Live Safely in a Science Fictional Universe

34

EL SOLDADO

"Uno, dos y tres el soldado p'al cuartel"

Daniel Villanueva waited until after dinner to tell Apá about the fight, about the *almost* fight. He stood in the doorway of his father's furniture workshop and tried telling him how he'd run away, but it was going all wrong. The small stand-alone garage—made mostly of rock and mortar—was busy with work, like it was almost every night after Apá finished eating and got started fixing the junk furniture he'd rescued from alleys and dumpsters around town. This second job the one Amá said was his dream. Outside there wasn't a cloud in the night sky, the stars above like pairs of unblinking eyes looking down to see what Apá was going to do after Daniel spilled his guts.

But Apá didn't take his attention from the dining room table he was restoring, continuing to stain the once busted legs he'd redesigned and replaced the night before, moving the brush up and down the curved fixtures in precise strokes. Apá was always like this. Hard working. Hard focused. Hard. Daniel inhaled the chemical smell of the dark cherry stain along with the scent of cut lumber and cigarette smoke. The single open window in the room not enough to clear the air.

"You should never run away," Apá said. He took a drag from the cigarette that had been burning in the ashtray beside him, the butt glowing. "Not from a fight."

"I wanted to do something, but I couldn't breathe." Daniel's brain had blanked after Adán shoved him in the middle of the chest, and all the air had rushed from his body. His thoughts had locked up like a seized engine. Apá's cheap little radio was playing in the background, Los Lobos's "La Pistola y el Corazón" buzzing faintly from the cracked speakers. The radio was on the corner of the worktable beside a box of nails and a hammer, by different sized chisels and handsaws. Everything covered in a layer of sawdust. *Y aquí siempre paso la vida con la pistola y el corazón; no se como amarte; no se como abrazarte; porque no se me deja este dolor que tengo yo.*

"You could breathe enough to run away," Apá said, raising an eyebrow. "Seems like running was *exactly* the something you wanted to do."

Daniel could feel the gaze of a billion stars on him but not a single one burning as hot as Apá's, who'd finally turned to look at him. The whites of his eyes were red, irritated by the smoke and chemicals in the air—the rest of him by Daniel. "If you say so," Daniel replied, wondering if his father would drop everything and chase him if he bolted. "I don't remember thinking nothing. I just ran."

Daniel's seventh-grade class had been at PE, divided into teams and made to play basketball. He'd spent most of the game trying to go unnoticed, to make it through without touching the ball or another person. But Adán Flores noticed him. He'd been watching Daniel as he ran back and forth along the sideline, staying somewhat close to the action but also keeping a safe distance, like the game was a swarm of bees he was trying to avoid. Adán was a classic bully, a kid who'd been held back a grade or two, was way bigger and stronger than everyone else but somehow terrible at sports—unless you counted fighting.

"You ran because you were scared," Apá told Daniel now. "That's what taking the easy way looks like. That's what running from a fight is. Being afraid makes you do the easy, and usually wrong, thing."

Adán had been missing baskets the entire game. The goon chucking the ball every time he got his hands on it. The game had gone so off the rails, his teammates quit passing to him and everything had slowed to an unenjoyable standstill. Seeming to get what was happening, Adán angrily snatched the ball from a teammate and dribbled directly toward Daniel, who'd been standing by the sideline at midcourt. Daniel saw him coming, Adán charging like a horse that had just tossed its rider and was now running free. But Daniel didn't move out of the way. Instead, he slightly turned, dropping his shoulder to absorb the impact as Adán lowered his.

Boom.

The two boys collided, and to Daniel's shock—and everyone else's—he wasn't knocked into outer space. Instead, he was only pushed back a few feet. Adán, however, was knocked backward, losing control of the ball and reaching wildly for it while trying to keep his balance. But he couldn't keep his feet and instead clumsily tripped and collapsed flat on his back, right onto the asphalt.

For a moment Daniel stood over Adán, not sure what to do as a crowd formed around them. He looked down at Adán—*stupid, stupid!*—guy's face was red. His eyes wet. Daniel quickly looked away as the laughing started.

Adán jumped to his feet and shoved Daniel square in the chest with the heels of his palms and immediately dropped him, leaving Daniel squirming on the blacktop. His eyes were pinched closed, and as he opened them, he saw Adán's red and black Pro Wings stepping toward him. Daniel was wearing the exact same pair. It was the brand of knockoff shoes poor parents bought for their poor kids, them looking sort of like a pair of Jordans but wearing like a kick-me sign. Daniel didn't remember getting to his feet or the look of rage and humiliation on Adán's face as he turned to run away. Not the roaring laughter of the crowd. Daniel didn't even realize he was running until he zipped past Señora Ramirez's, kicking up the perfectly manicured gravel of her front yard.

"I'm going to teach you to never run away again," Apá continued. He put his brush down and lit another cigarette, took a long drag before exhaling. A twist of smoke curled in the air between them. Apá wasn't looking at Daniel as he spoke, instead focusing on the still unfinished chairs stacked in the corner of the room. "I learned how to be a warrior when I was your age. It's how I made it in the army. How I make it now."

"Who are you out there fighting *now*?" Daniel couldn't keep from asking. "Those chairs?"

"Being a warrior is about doing the hard thing every time," Apá said, blowing a cloud of smoke and shaking his head. "It's not always about actual fighting." He mashed the cigarette into the crowded ashtray and looked hard at Daniel. Sweat soaked through the bandanna he wore to keep it from rolling into his eyes. His hands were dry and cracked. His face with spots cooked in from the sun.

"Okay, Apá," Daniel said, relief coating his body like a film. "That's good to hear."

"I mean, don't get confused," Apá said. "Because sometimes it *is*, and tomorrow you're fighting that boy." The room turned as silent as a graveyard, minus Apá's tiny radio.

No se como decirte; no se como explicarte; que aquí no hay remedio.

Daniel wondered how he was going to learn to fight in one night. To become a warrior. Apá had been in the army, but he never talked about it. He never talked about anything. How could he teach him to fight? How could he teach him *anything*?

CHAPTER ONE

DANNY THE FISH

No way was Danny Villanueva going to learn a thing. At least not sitting in art class. Danny fidgeted in his seat as his fellow Intro to Basic Drawing students scribbled in their notebooks. Danny's most recent piece—*The Hallway*—had been placed front and center of the room, propped on a big wooden easel for everyone to take in. He'd quickly sketched it the night before it was due and ripped it from his spiral art book before turning it in, the little perforated ends still dangling from its side. Danny couldn't bear to look at the piece now, the hallway looking like it had been drawn by someone who'd never actually stood inside one before. There was no door at the end of the long, narrow passageway. In fact, there were no doors at all. On one wall there was a pair of tiny windows drawn side by side, and the other was bare. Danny wondered what kind of building this hallway could exist in—if it had reason to exist at all, other than to fail an art class. Danny looked out the classroom window. His car was only a few hundred yards away, illegally parked by a fire hydrant in front of the Student Union. Fleeing from class was a better choice than staying. He could avoid a ticket *and* humiliation. Why stick around for that, other than the class participation points. *Obviously.*

Pablo, his art professor, had made that a major part of everyone's grade. He had broken the class down into two parts. Technique and critique. The first half was *technique*, drawing exercises like sketching circles and cubes, pairs of hands and flowers. Pairs of hands holding flowers. These in-class assignments were almost always pencil-drawn images meant to develop shading techniques and crosshatching, detail work and tonal sketching—*boring, easy stuff*—followed by a take-home piece. And after that was *critique*, where the class discussed Pablo's take-home assignment, which would end up as part of their end-of-semester portfolio. *The Hallway* was Danny's third, and last, piece of the semester. It was also his worst. Much worse than the hands and the flowers he'd turned in last week. But just by talking in class—discussing the work, as Pablo like to say—they could make up a third of their grade. All Danny had to do was remain silent as the class beat up his hallway and then chatted up the remaining assignments. *Easy.*

Pablo moved toward the front of the room, his arms folded across his chest as he studied Danny's hallway. Way back on the first day of class, Danny thought his new art professor was going to be cool, him telling everyone, *Call me Pablo*, like he was not going to be grading them. Like now, he'd been wearing a too tight T-shirt and ripped-up jeans, a pair of scuzzy

Chucks. If only the Sarge—Danny's father—could've seen him. He would have wondered what he'd just spent all that tuition money on. Why the guy couldn't bother to wear a tie or at least a collared shirt.

Now in December and coming toward the end of the semester, that morning seemed like forever ago. As did Danny's hopes of doing better in college than he'd done in high school. Danny's report cards were routinely more down than up, but he'd always blamed it on being an army brat and bouncing around high schools, even after settling in El Paso permanently. He had promised the Sarge—and himself—that everything would come together when he started college. That he wouldn't waste all the money the Sarge had forked out for that and room and board. A future.

Thing was Danny had been sure that everything *would* come together, was confident during student orientation at UTEP. He'd never found actual classroom work hard. Maybe not always interesting—sometimes boring as hell—but he never felt totally out of place, like if a dog had been enrolled in a cooking class and was expected to bake a cake. But he was screwing up pretty bad in biology and needed extra credit there, too. The class had hundreds of students and no way did Dr. A even know his name, which made requesting extra credit feel like asking a stranger to borrow underwear. And he was just hanging on in Econ and English.

"Last week we talked about having a focal point in our work," Pablo was saying, surveying the room. "That our pieces should draw the eye, an observer's attention."

"This is like a hallway to nowhere," Jason said, chinning

toward Danny's drawing. Jason was the guy in class who never raised his hand to talk but who talked all the time.

"Yeah," Erika chimed in, her hand waving in the air. "But, like, in a bad way." She pulled her hand down and continued. "I can see that he was going for, like, a minimalist thing, but it just doesn't work."

Pablo nodded as she spoke, considering what she'd said. "Let's try to avoid words like *good* and *bad* and talk about what is on the page itself." He now addressed the rest of the room. There was a silence. Truth? Danny had forgotten all about the hallway assignment almost immediately after it had been handed out. Lately he'd been having a hard time keeping track of a lot of things. He had two half-written essays open on his laptop, both due soon but he wasn't sure when. Finals were coming, but he had the exact days and times confused. He'd also completely forgotten about JD's—his best friend—birthday.

"The black-and-white tile floor is working," came a voice from the back of the class. "The shading on those is well done." Natalia hardly ever said anything in class, but her work was pretty dope. So maybe she didn't need the points.

"I thought they were cliché," Jason argued, turning to face Natalia. "And Pablo is right. There is nothing in the piece that draws my attention. My eyes don't know where to go."

How hard *was* he supposed to bite his tongue? Danny wondered. And would his death be considered a suicide or an accident if he bit it off and choked to death? And that's when he lost it. "You know what's cliché?" Danny snapped. "How thirsty you're being for this fucking art teacher's approval. Like anyone even cares. He don't."

"Danny Villanueva!" Pablo barked. "What the hell?"

Danny could feel the room suddenly staring at him. He looked directly at his hallway. It hadn't taken more than fifteen minutes to draw, all the lines slightly crooked and rushed. He could see where he'd been sloppy, where his hand had smeared some of the tiles along the bottom of the page. There was no use of any real skill. Of detail. Of give-a-shit.

"You know I'm right!" Danny said anyway. "He's faking like some pretentious art critic. He's doing that just for you, homes." There was a collective gasp in the room, followed by another, more stifling silence. It was as if all the air in the room had been sucked away.

"No," Pablo corrected. "Jason was participating in class, and you are violating the student code of conduct."

"Whatever." Danny slumped down in his seat. "The assignment was to draw a hallway, not a masterpiece."

"Not another word." Pablo jabbed a finger in Danny's direction. "You are going to leave the class right now. You are going to walk to my office, and you are going to sit and wait until I get there. Do you understand?"

Danny looked at Pablo, the expression on his face stern and serious as fuck. So he nodded quickly, quietly packed up his stuff, and bolted from the room, not looking back as he closed the door behind him.

Danny's class was inside the same massive building where concert performances were held, where student art was also shown, a modern space with gleaming white paneled walls and a glossy tile floor called the Glass Gallery. Danny often stopped by to check out paintings, the pieces expertly hung as if they were priceless works in a museum and not student projects. He sometimes felt guilty for not really wanting to *see* the work, instead more interested in knowing why someone thought what was here was good enough for the wall space.

The complex also housed the depressingly named Beehive, where Danny was now heading. The Beehive was a collection of cubicles where the college kept its worker bees—the part-time adjuncts. At the entrance was a table with pamphlets spread across it, tri-folds with weird titles like *Get It Up! How to Improve Your GPA*, *Is This Your First Time? A Freshman Guide to Campus Life*, and *Friends with Benefits: Study Groups and You.*

Danny—feeling shaky after what had happened in class—grabbed one as he turned the corner into a phalanx of cubicle dividers spreading across a large room. The Beehive could easily be confused for a call center or giant test lab where scientists studied the effects of sadness and boredom on people who once had dreams. Danny looked at his pamphlet:

TOP FIVE STUDY TIPS FOR THE STRUGGLING STUDENT

1. Schedule time to study. Did you know actually studying is the number one way to get better at studying?
2. Find a study partner. Make a friend, you loser. If you can't make a friend here, can you even?
3. Avoid distractions. Are you still dreaming about painting on walls? That's a crime, not art.

4. Have you tried trying?
5. Always remember how hard everyone has worked for you. Remember that criticism is a gift. Remember all the gifts you've been given.

There was another teacher in Pod B2, hunched over her phone, tapping away. She was younger than Pablo, had punky blue-black hair and stylish big-framed glasses. Seeing her made Danny wonder how long Pablo had been teaching. How much cubby time he'd logged. There were two other desks with empty chairs neatly placed at them in the pod, the teachers somewhere else, but their little tchotchkes, coffee mugs with pens jammed in them, picture frames with smiling strangers inside, little daily calendars remained.

There was nothing on Pablo's desk.

Danny grabbed an empty chair and nervously poked at his phone. He wondered what Pablo was going to tell him when he arrived. He'd looked pissed standing beside Danny's homework, and that was before Danny'd said a peep to Jason. There was a good chance, Danny decided, that he was about to get tossed from the class. He vaguely remembered hearing something about the student code of conduct during orientation, a student volunteer saying it was online. He briefly thought about looking it up but decided nah. Pablo would just tell him. He seemed like the Sarge in that way. Probably loved giving bad news.

"Bro, why are you like that?" Pablo said, fixing a stare at Danny as he rushed inside the pod a second later. He tossed his old-timey-looking satchel onto the empty desk and sank into the chair beside Danny. It was the kind of bag only a hipster artist—or a mailman from the Wild West days—would carry. Pablo shook his head in disbelief as he continued to stare, as if he hadn't stopped thinking about the incident since it happened.

"Why am I like what?" Danny asked, knowing exactly what Pablo meant. People like Jason and Erika put him on edge. His entire senior year at Cathedral, a private Catholic school Danny went to after getting expelled from his old high school, was full of Jasons. The Sarge telling him the experience was finally going to prepare him for college—so much for that!

"An asshole," Pablo answered. The other teacher in the cubicle stopped tapping on her phone and turned to look at Pablo, her big brown eyes narrowing on him like lasers. Pablo smiled apologetically at her until she turned her attention back to her phone. He then reached for his satchel and pulled out a sketchbook. The cover was worn, lots of trips in and out of the bag. Pencil lead stains marked the edges. He thumped the side and studied Danny. "Put your phone down."

Danny had been holding it, an automatic habit. He looked down at the blank phone screen in his lap and then back at Pablo. He wasn't acting like he was going to toss him from class, at least not yet. So he placed his phone on Pablo's desk.

"Look," Pablo continued. "I don't want to waste my time on a kid who's got it but doesn't get it."

"I'll redo the hallway," Danny said quickly. "I'll do whatever. I need to pass, okay?"

"That's the problem. You're already doing whatever."

Pablo opened the sketchbook and, half turning it to Danny, flipped through it, drawings of ordinary still lifes, of a murder of crows in the twisted branches of a huizache, jagged mountains cutting across the desert sky, a nopal in bloom skipped by. Pablo then stopped on an image of a boy. It was a portrait. The kid, maybe five or six, was facing away, his back at an angle, his shoulders raised like he was walking away but stopped, as if spooked and ready to suddenly spin around. The boy's face was in profile, about to glance at what was behind him. His expression wasn't quite scared, more the second right before fear, before realizing he was all by himself.

"Do you know what all these pieces have in common?" Pablo continued as Danny's phone buzzed, the black screen lighting up.

"No." Danny didn't know what Pablo was getting at, but the motherfucker could draw. He looked over at his phone. MÁ MISSED CALL.

"I care about each drawing," Pablo said. "It's that simple. I care about what I'm making."

"No one cares about hallways," Danny said, knowing he sounded more defensive than he wanted to.

"No, *you* didn't care about hallways. First, a hallway can be anything. Endless possibilities. You could've made the assignment anything you wanted it to be, and you simply failed. Second, you don't care about other people's feelings or opinions. You failed at being a decent person to your fellow classmates. Do you even get that?"

"Yes." And he did. He felt embarrassed and desperately wanted to apologize. And not just to Jason but everyone, especially Natalia, who was trying to be nice even though his work was trash. *Good job, idiot.*

"You don't seem to care about this art class, and *that* is why you're failing." Pablo closed his sketchbook and again tapped the cover with his finger. "You have the technical skills. I've seen them when we do our exercises in class. I know tons of artists like you, with all the ability in the world but not a drop of courage to make yourself, or someone else, care."

Danny shifted uncomfortably. He was surprised to know that Pablo thought he had any talent at all. That he considered him an artist.

"Then let me do what I care about," he said, the words escaping his mouth before he could think about them. Things Danny cared about had a way of vanishing on him. It made caring a gamble.

His phone started ringing again, his má calling for the second time, which was super unusual. But again he didn't reach to answer it. Instead, he and Pablo looked at the glowing image on the screen. The drawing was one Danny had painted on his tablet, something he maybe wanted to make a mural of someday. The image was of a skeleton dressed as a cop, its uniform a crisp and deep blue, the bony face hidden behind a pair of mirrored sunglasses. The painting was a recreated Lotería card, La Muerte, standing out against a faded pink background. Death's badge painted silver and shiny, exactly like its scythe.

"Now, *that* is pretty good," Pablo said, leaning forward. "Tell me about that."

"I painted it on my tablet." Danny hesitated, then added

in a rush, "I did it a little bit after a cop shot and killed my friend."

"That happen in Central, right?" Pablo asked, his face wrinkling, like a memory was coming to him. "Maybe a year ago?"

"Yeah." Danny didn't say more, didn't want to.

Juan's killing was all over the local news and online right after it happened. All the articles told the basic story. JD and Juan were trespassing at this old apartment complex in Central and that Juan had had a gun, the police killing him behind the building. None of the stories mentioned how Juan was on his way to see his father for the first time. That JD was helping him drive across the state in a *borrowed* truck, Fabi's—Juan's mom. The gun had been hers, hidden under the seat. They didn't want to get busted driving with a gun, so they'd gone to ditch it behind the apartment complex. The boys having no idea what would happen next.

"Do you play Lotería?" Pablo caught on, shifted the conversation. "Me and my family used to play all the time. The games used to get pretty heated. It's a good time."

"I've never played," Danny said simply. "My friend's mom gave the stack of cards to me. I just liked the art."

The Sarge, Má, and Danny had gone to see Fabi a few days after Juan's funeral, Má making a pot of birria along with corn tortillas for her. Má and the Sarge disappeared into the house almost as soon as they arrived, carrying the pot and all the extra stuff: salsa and diced onions, cut limes. Danny stayed on the porch and watched as Juan's grandpa took inventory of the front yard, making a list of the car and washing machine parts. The milk crates with jars half-filled with random nuts and bolts.

Fabi joined Danny on the porch, carrying a cardboard box labeled DONATIONS. She put it down on the little table—two metal folding chairs pushed neatly underneath—beside the front door. Danny watched as Juan's grandpa continued making notes on a scrap of paper. "I have a guy coming tomorrow to haul all that crap away," Fabi told him. "We're moving far the hell away and not taking a single screw."

Danny had looked inside the box and saw the Lotería cards. La Muerte was on top. Number fourteen. He had seen this image of Death before. The reaper on shirts or hats being sold at the swap meet, though he wasn't sure where this particular one came from. He looked back at Fabi, who was now smiling at him, and the look on her face made him want to cry. She was thinking of Juan, just like he was. Hearing Fabi's voice. Smelling Juan's house. Watching Juan's grandpa count all the familiar junk that was going to disappear the next day was punching a hole right through Danny's heart.

"Do you want them?" Fabi asked.

"What are they?"

"It's a game. Kind of like bingo." Fabi rummaged through the box, pulled out a tabla and a set of instructions with a description of all fifty-four cards. The tablet had sixteen images, four up and down, four across. "Someone shuffles the deck and then flips the cards over and calls them out. The person can say the little phrases or whatever. You get four in a row, you win. Not too complicated."

"You ever play with Juan?" Danny asked.

"Nah. A bartender friend at the bar I worked at used these like tarots." She grabbed the stack and motioned for Danny to take a seat as she joined him. Fabi began shuffling. "I never used them, but I liked watching her work." Watching her shuffle the small deck with ease, Danny didn't believe for a second that she wasn't the bartender psychic. Fabi set four cards facedown in front of Danny and looked at him with a mysteriously grave expression. "My friend would tell whoever she was reading that the cards could not predict the future. Only the past."

"What is that supposed to mean?" Danny said, trying not to laugh.

Fabi shifted in her seat, her posture straightening. She reached across the table and squeezed Danny's hand. "It means the past is still happening, dummy."

Danny could feel a lump in his throat growing as Fabi smiled at him again. She seemed hollow, as empty as her home was now becoming, box by box. She sat back and contemplated the four cards. She slowly reached for the first and flipped it over. Number fifty, El Pescado. Danny gawked at the image, a fish being yanked from the water, a giant hook in its mouth.

"El que por la boca muere," she continued, her voice softer but not comforting.

"What the fuck is *that* supposed to mean?"

"Nothing." Fabi stifled a laugh as she scooped up the cards without flipping the rest over. "She's a fucking bartender. Her job was to get people drunk, listen to their sins, and hopefully get tipped like crazy." Fabi stacked the cards, the tabla, and instructions neatly beside her box of donations. "Don't pay any attention to that card," Fabi continued. "Or to me. Juanito always said you talked crazy, but he liked that about you."

Danny could see a lot of Juan in her face, in her expressions as she tried to make him feel better. Danny wasn't so sure talking crazy would ever do him any good, but he also didn't believe in Lotería card psychics. "Maybe I should get drunk" is what he said instead.

"Well, you're not doing that here," Fabi said, standing to leave. "But you can keep the cards."

Pablo was rubbing his face like a game show contestant thinking over a doozy of a question. "I've always liked the art too. How many of these have you done?"

"Just the reaper cop," Danny said. He'd finished it the same day he'd visited Fabi, actually. After thinking about her card reading and how, like pescado, his mouth had again gotten him into trouble.

"Okay, look. You don't have a lot of time," Pablo said, nodding as if coming to some decision. "If you want to pass the class, I want three new Lotería paintings for your portfolio. If you can do that and they're good—if they look like you actually put heart into them—you'll make it. You'll pass the class."

"But this is a drawing class," Danny said.

"Like you said, it's an art class."

Danny's phone buzzed again. This time it was a text message. Both Danny and Pablo turned to read it. It was from Má.

I don't know what you're doing, but you need to get

to Beaumont right now. Your dad collapsed. He's unconscious. We're in the ambulance.

"I gotta go," Danny said, jumping to his feet, jamming his phone and the image of La Muerte back inside his pocket. "It's my dad." A sense of alarm grew quickly inside his body, his own internal sirens going off. Sirens of panic. Regret. Dread.

CHAPTER TWO

POP QUIZ

Just seeing the bomb filled JD with dread. A single five hundred pounder with sharp protruding tail fins and a bottle-shape nose rested on an unassuming trailer beside the A-10. Before joining the air force, JD wouldn't have been able to name a single military airplane. But now he could, *the A-10!* It was the only jet JD loaded with bombs at Davis-Monthan—the air force base located in the middle of Tucson and where he'd been stationed for the past three months. The trailer had been pulled inside the aircraft hangar and sat beside the jet so JD—along with his crew—could prove he could load it onto the plane.

"I thought after high school I'd be all done with pop quizzes," JD griped. "I don't get why they're making me do this." JD had never been good with tests. With surprises. Staff Sergeant Phil Rowe, JD's boss and head of the crew, had startled JD earlier that morning, yelling at him over the phone to come back to work ASAP, even though JD had just gotten off shift three hours earlier. Pop quiz time, air force style. Rowe explained that the crew *had* to pass the load on the very first try, that everything needed to go smoothly and everyone had to look in sync—like they'd been working together for years instead of months. When JD asked why that mattered, Rowe snapped, *Don't worry about it*, and quickly hung up.

"Quit bitching and grab your tools," Rowe said now. "You're getting on my nerves." JD was getting on *his* nerves? Rowe was an *irritating* motherfucker, always flapping his gums on the flight line or in the shop about politics and religion, music or sports. He'd grown up in some swamp in Florida and never shut up about airboats and gators, hunting and fishing. Even when he wasn't talking, the lunatic hummed and whistled. The dude was incapable of not making noise.

JD stuffed his speed handle, sockets and ratchets, and a handful of wrenches into his green tool bag. Whether he was irritating or not, JD needed to listen to him. Not only was Rowe his boss, but he'd been loading bombs and fixing airplanes for *a decade*—the man halfway to a twenty-year retirement. JD had only turned nineteen a week ago—not that anyone noticed or cared. JD couldn't for a second imagine the weirdness of one day working side by side with his little brother, Tomásito, who ever since turning ten would only answer to Tomás.

"I'm not bitching," JD said, turning to Raines, the third member of their three-man crew. "Am I?" JD couldn't help but feel like he was being messed with, and not just by Rowe but also Hermosillo. Master Sergeant Hermosillo was the flight chief and Rowe's boss. The dude would've made the perfect high school assistant principal, an equal mix of always busy and always angry.

Raines walked away from Rowe and JD without bothering to answer. *Classic Raines.* He was heading toward the jammer. Like the trailer, it was painted a flat green, a cross between a forklift and a go-cart. JD wished his job had been to drive the jammer, but he'd gotten stuck taking care of the toolbox. And those were basically the jobs for their three-person crew. Rowe was the boss. Raines drove the jammer. And JD took care of the tools.

At least Darius Raines was cool, a senior airman finishing his first enlistment—he had only a year and change left and was *done.* Raines was from LA, and so JD—who wanted to be a movie director more than *anything*—was always hitting him with questions. *Did you ever see movies being made on location? Did you go watch? Did you visit any of the studios? Do you know anyone who works there? Can you introduce me?* Raines was the exact opposite of Rowe. A quiet, thoughtful guy who answered JD's questions but otherwise didn't talk all that much. Raines had a wife and a new baby, and he wasn't *ever* moving back to California. He planned on staying in Tucson when he got out and had already bought a house. Raines would shake his head and *tsk-tsk* whenever JD told him his plans about moving to LA and one day making movies. G*ood luck with that. I'll watch them from here.*

The LSC crew walked out of their office, which meant it was time to start. The Load Standardization Crew's job was to certify load crews like JD's to install bombs and missiles on airplanes by making sure the crew exactingly followed a checklist of over two hundred steps without missing a single one. A load crew was supposed to work like a well-oiled machine, to be like the Three Musketeers. All for one and one for all—or some shit like that. But after being in the shop, it seemed like some crews were more like the Three Amigos. Guys who joined expecting one thing but getting another. Others were the Stooges, funny but not always on purpose.

In high school JD had spent most of his time kicking it with Juan and Danny, his two best friends. The three of them spent a bunch of time in Central El Paso. Walking back and forth to each other's houses. Buying cigarettes and 40s at the liquor store. And ballin'. Especially Juan and JD. JD played so much that shooting a basketball felt as easy as snapping his fingers. Now, *they'd* been a crew. JD still couldn't wrap his mind around the fact that at any one moment Juan wasn't somewhere alive in the world. That he was just *dead*. At least Danny was a college boy now, which was something he was always going to be. *Good for him*. JD was happy things were going to work out for Danny, like always, even if it meant Danny would eventually forget all about him, starting with his birthday last week.

"Line it up," Rowe barked as JD stood in front of the toolbox, Raines joining him. There was a lot of formality to the certification process, Rowe having to brief his crew about the different risks and dangers before they started, which they already knew inside out, reading from a checklist they had to follow. They could accidentally blow themselves up. Slice their fingers or hands off. Get crushed. Of course the bomb they were loading onto the A-10 wasn't live, but they had to treat it as if it were, because one day it would be. And the inert bomb was still dangerous.

The LSC crew watched, arms folded, as Rowe stumbled over his brief, his voice halting and hesitant as he read aloud from the checklist. JD had never seem Rowe nervous before, looking suddenly ready to fold under the pressure, the LSC crew suddenly Olympic judges scoring some once-in-a-lifetime event. The load was timed—twenty-five minutes—and any safety violations were an automatic fail, and style points absolutely mattered. A load could be stopped at any time for a lack of proficiency. This, JD got. Working jets felt a lot like basketball practice. Coach Paul would make the team run the same plays over and over. JD used to hate it, the repetition so boring. The constant setting of picks and boxing out. The passing and shooting drills. The over and over of every detail. The drills used to make the game seem so small. Until game time.

"You guys ready?" Rowe asked after his brief. As if there were more than one answer. Raines stared straight ahead—looking ready—and JD nodded. "Okay then. Break."

They sprang into action.

Raines approached the bomb and looked it over, gently tugged the safety devices securing the spring-loaded fins that would fully open once the weapon was released in flight. Rowe stood by the front of the A-10, scanning his checklist as JD circled the jet, making sure it was safe to work on. That the aircraft was grounded and that a long metal cord ran from the plane to a metal lug in the ground, dissipating any static electricity and the chances of frying electrical parts or setting off explosives.

Satisfied the bomb was secured, Raines cranked up the jammer, the motor loudly coughing to life as a cloud of black smoke rolled into the air. Rowe headed over to the bomb trailer. So far, JD knew they looked like they'd been loading together for years, not months. The LSC crew stood off to the side, heads nodding in approval at different times depending on what they were watching, scribbling in their notebooks.

Then JD noticed Hermosillo was there watching as Rowe and Raines had the bomb raised from the trailer. The distraction made JD late getting over to them. He needed to do the weight check, a little tug of the tail fin to make sure all the weight was transferred from the trailer and to the jammer. That they weren't about to drop it. Rowe glared as JD rushed over and gently pushed up and down on the tail fin.

Rowe nodded at Raines—it was good—and then *he* noticed Hermosillo watching. His face turned red, and JD looked away. Raines raised the jammer's hydraulic arms and inched the bomb off the trailer just enough for Rowe to be able to strap it to the lift truck with a thick nylon tie-down. JD could feel Rowe mad-dogging him as he gripped the tail of the bomb. He thought of how easy it was to fall behind in a game of basketball, how one bad play morphed into two, how two spiraled into three until the score was a lopsided mess.

Raines pulled away from the trailer and drove slowly toward the airplane, JD holding the bomb by the tail. He hated feeling the free weight of the bomb beside him. He ducked underneath the plane's wing and toward the hardpoint, where the bomb would be attached. It was up to him to guide the bomb in smoothly so Rowe could lock it in place. He and Raines had done it about a million times before Rowe had been satisfied. *This* took practice. Like free throws, the motion seemingly easy but not entirely natural—especially now with people watching.

"Are you blind?" Rowe yelled over the putting engine of the jammer. "You're crooked as fuck." He was yelling at Raines, who shot a look at JD. Raines was right. JD hadn't guided him straight. But Rowe hadn't been paying attention either. He should've noticed earlier, instead of going over his checklist. Hermosillo widened his stance as he continued to look on. The well-oiled machine of only a few moments ago was breaking down. *How many bad plays was that?*

Like on the basketball court, a team needed to talk, or it was toast. "My bad," JD yelled, motioning to Raines to back up and come in again. "Let's run it again!" Raines nodded, put the jammer in reverse and slowly backed up. JD walked the bomb back out from underneath the jet. Even though it was mid-December and cold, he was sweating, a slick layer coating his body and running down his back. And he was wiped from working the night before and this whole situation felt like some fourth-quarter type shit. The moments his old coach was always preparing the team for. The ones Juan played in while JD mostly watched from the bench. Only JD wasn't on the bench now.

And they could still pass this load. JD was sure of it.

But Hermosillo and LSC had too much real estate in Rowe's head. He was now dividing his attention between his checklist and his evaluators, as if the *what the fuck are you doing?* looks on their faces were going to suddenly transform into attaboy smiles.

JD and Raines reapproached the plane, JD aligning the bomb perfectly with the hardpoint. This time all Rowe had to do was take his ratchet and lock the bomb in. Game over.

JD and Raines sat uneasily in the ready room outside Hermosillo's office as a couple of day shifters—Curtain and Peterson—wolfed down lunch. The ready room was sort of like a break room, a space with tables and chairs. A microwave stashed in the corner, along with an industrial-size fridge. Maintainers of all types were always coming and going. Crew chiefs and avionics troops. Electricians and weapons. Sure, they ate lunches and took breaks, but mostly they wrote in dispatch logs or typed away at computer terminals stationed along the walls. The ready room was for documenting jobs done on the airplanes and to stand by for more.

"How long has he been in with the boss?" Curtain asked, referring to Rowe. Curtain was an airman like JD and had been the newest guy in the shop before JD arrived. JD still remembered their first conversation:

> *Now you're the FNG, Curtain said, looking excited to see JD on his first day.*
> *What's that? JD said, relieved that someone looked glad to meet him; everyone else looking bored or annoyed at the sight of him.*
> *Shut up Fucking New Guy.*

JD shifted in his seat. "Like twenty minutes maybe," he said. "Him, LSC, and Hermosillo all disappeared after the load."

"So you failed?" Curtain said.

"Pretty sure," JD said. "LSC said we fail and pass as a crew. So yeah."

"Calm down, Corporate," Raines cut in. "Rowe fucked up like he always does."

"He fail the checklist again?" Curtain asked Raines.

"You know it." Raines shrugged. "Didn't mark off a bunch of steps."

"They're not gonna let him go," Peterson said. "And he wants it so bad, too."

"I'm sure he's telling the boss the checklist is rigged or some shit," Curtain joked. "Anything to let him go."

Curtain was an airman first class who talked shit at a staff sergeant level. Him and Peterson were in their twenties and liked to party. Had cool-ass cars. Good sneaker game.

That was when it dawned on him what they'd just said. "Not gonna let Rowe go where?" JD turned to Raines, the look on his face growing hard.

"Nowhere," Raines said, an edge in his voice. "Ain't that right, guys?"

"Take it easy," Peterson said. "Jesus." He turned to JD. "Your boss can't figure out a checklist, so they decertified him last year. *But* we're short on people—because dudes like your boy over here keep getting out—so they wanna see if, *magically*, Rowe don't suck now."

"Don't blame me for this nonsense," Raines said, hands up in protest. "I'm just doing my time and rolling. No more, no less."

JD got that. He'd signed up for the air force barely a week after Juan's funeral, took the first slot leaving after graduation, not thinking jobs at all. What he was after was college money, a shot at film school—and if he was being honest, he was also after getting as far away from where Juan was killed, from his parents' divorce, and his old man's *new* old lady, as he could.

But like Raines, JD planned on doing his four and bouncing, even if he was sort of digging being a maintainer. The night before, an aircraft had come back broke, the gun system not rotating in flight. JD worked the jet with another crew and carefully read the fault isolation manual, followed the troubleshooting tree, and tested the wiring on the airplane until he found a bad hydraulic motor. He could fix a *jet*, man. Felt surprisingly good, finding the problem and repairing it with his own hands.

A TV flicked on behind JD as another group of crew chiefs sat down at the table beside them.

"What you got going after work?" Curtain asked. "We're gonna play some NBA 2K and drink some beers. You should come by."

"I'm pretty wiped out," JD said. Truth. His entire body ached. *When was the last time he'd eaten?* He routinely worked long shifts, his scheduled eight-hour days frequently turning into twelve and fourteen, but the last twenty-four had been brutal. "After this"—he cocked his head toward the door—"I'm gonna go for a run and crash."

"The running part don't make no sense," Peterson said. "But for sure passing out."

"Maybe tomorrow?" Curtain said. "We're gonna hit up the bars on University."

"He ain't doing that," Raines answered for JD. "He's a kid."

"If he's here, he ain't no kid," Peterson said. "Sanchez, why don't you ever come out with us?"

"That's not true," JD lied. But it pretty much was. In the past three months JD had hung out with the guys from the shop only twice. They'd been cool, inviting him to hang in the dorms. To go out in town.

"What about tomorrow, then?"

"Aren't you going to El Paso?" Raines asked JD. "You should leave tonight. I bet Hermosillo would let you."

Peterson frowned. "Are you like his dad or something?"

"He ain't, but I am," Rowe said, storming into the ready room and interrupting. They all turned to look at him. Behind Rowe were muted images of a mountain range. The evening sky pinkish with thin clouds seemed perfect for a cheesy vacation destination commercial, when a bomb suddenly exploded along a ridge. The camera went shaky as more explosions flashed. *One. Two. Three.* Then nothing. The camera went off before the image repeated itself. "And he ain't going nowhere tonight. We got load barn in the morning."

"Are you fucking kidding me?" Raines said, looking past Rowe and into Hermosillo's office. The door was closed. "Where's the boss?"

"*I'm* your boss. And you two fucked up today." Rowe looked directly at JD as he said this. "And if we don't pass tomorrow, you ain't leaving this base. Your time off is as good as canceled. So you better not fuck up."

"Are you serious?" JD asked.

"As serious as a bomb," Rowe said, his finger now pointing in JD's face. "As serious as a motherfucking bomb."

JD sat in his dorm room dressed for a run in his bright blue Hokas and matching shorts. A thin blue hoodie. He had to hurry if he wanted to still make it to the mountain before the sun went down. Normally he went for long runs like this on the weekends, but the plan was to be in El Paso and there'd be no time for ten milers.

He'd gotten into running by accident. Technical Sergeant Bullard, his recruiter, had told JD that he needed to be in shape for basic training, to be able to run a mile and a half. So JD had started running and almost immediately fell in love with it, with the sounds of his feet crunching the dirt underneath him. The in and out of his breath. As he ran, his body felt like a grandfather clock keeping time, his movements like seconds ticking away.

Running was when his head was also the clearest and movie ideas came to him in flashes.

And he thought about movies all the time. The walls of his dorm room were covered with framed posters from films he loved. The animated, alternate version of *Pan's Labyrinth*, with its green and gold background and floating sprites. His multiple versions of Everything Everywhere All at Once were hung perfectly side by side above his bed. There was a signed *Amores Perros* poster, Alejandro González Iñárritu's name scrawled across the title. JD was making money for the first time in his life, and the cash *was* making him happy. Had a new computer with real-deal editing software. An iPhone with a camera that could shoot footage like a pro. He'd been reading books on filmmaking. Editing. Screenwriting. He'd do his time here, and then it was going to be all about film school, learning the craft. No way would he ever be some sucker with bad gear again.

For sure not the sucker he'd been last year, when a shitty camera helped ruin the documentary he was making. Going over the footage on his laptop, which he always found himself doing whenever thinking of El Paso or going home, JD dragged the cursor and watched the screen again. They'd been at Danny's the night Juan died—him and Juan, Danny—at a little kickback before hitting the road to meet Juan's father. Juan had the big game coming up in a week, his one chance for a basketball scholarship. The Panasonic had needed way more light, but JD didn't know that then, and everything on the screen had come out dark. The sound sucked, too. What he'd recorded looked like bad security cam footage, and he would have deleted it if Juan's voice and shadowy image weren't still there for him to look at whenever he wanted.

Juan and Danny were having a good time in the frames. Talking shit. Drinking 40s. JD frowned at the clip—he should've been doing the same. It was the last time all three of them were together, and instead, he'd been tied in knots. He'd just accidentally exposed his old man's affair. Caused his family to break apart. He'd also totaled his car and gotten kicked off the basketball team. He couldn't imagine things sucking harder. He shook his head at how stupid he'd been, because an hour later he would watch his best friend be shot and killed in front of him.

He wondered if it was still being stupid, planning to make the five-hour drive to El Paso this weekend and hoping to have fun. His birthday was earlier in the week, and no one really noticed. Amá had called, saying it would've been better to wish him a happy birthday in person, but the tone of her voice didn't really match her words. She was still mad that he'd joined the military. His sister Alma texted. Danny texted too, but two days late. He'd told JD to come down, to stay with him and they'd kick it like back in the day. He dragged the cursor back one more time and listen to Danny and Juan laughing.

Pops hadn't called or texted at all. Nothing.

JD closed the video file, leaving the screenplay he was writing on the screen. He'd been researching protagonists and antagonists. Three-act structures. Beginnings. Middles. Ends.

He shut the laptop, knowing that he needed to run.

To get to that mountain.

JUAN LAST CHANCE

ACT ONE

"THE VULTURE"

EXT. DESERT MOUNTAIN TRAIL-MAGIC HOUR

Saguaro cactus line the side of the mountain in the distance. Above the sky is orange and purple, thin white clouds stretching above. The sound of footsteps CRUNCHING on dirt can be heard as a narrow trail cuts through nopales, yuccas, creosote, and more towering bright green saguaros.

JD is running along the trail, dressed just as brightly as the cactus in garish bright blue running gear—matching blue shoes, shorts, and hoodie. AirPods are fixed in his ears. He can't hear the YIPS of coyotes in the distance as he moves along. Above him, a vulture circles.

The bird's wingspan is impressive as it glides through the air above JD and then swoops down toward the trail ahead. Disappearing into the desert.

EXT. EL PASO/NEIGHBORHOOD-EVENING

Cut to a close-up of a green street sign, PIEDRAS AVE. A traffic light glows red and backs up a mix of old beaters and stylish rides. The surrounding neighborhood is older, some storefronts boarded up, but there are signs of life. Newer, hipper shops with fresh coats of paint alongside neighborhood standbys. A yoga studio next to a shoe repair shop. A vegan eatery next to a plumbing parts place.

POPS and SONYA are waiting at the crosswalk, Pops staring hard at the red light. Little stone and brick houses are off in the distance. Like Pops and Sonya, couples are out and about. As are KIDS riding bikes. Packs of TEENS. The UNHOUSED pushing overstuffed shopping carts.

SONYA

Mi amor, you can't look red lights into changing.
The light turned green and Pops turns to Sonya, raising an eyebrow.

POPS
(grinning)
Don't tell me what I can't do
with my looks.

The couple laughs and then quickly kisses as they cross the street. But Sonya's face turns serious once they make it across. She takes Pops's hand in hers.

SONYA
Have you called him yet?

POPS
(exasperated)
Mi amor. I don't think I'm going
to.

SONYA
But it's our wedding. You need
to invite someone from your
family. You don't want people
thinking you're some kind of
weird loner. Besides, he's not a
boy, right? Treat him like a man.

Pops starts walking, gently pulling Sonya along.

CUT TO:

EXT. POPS'S HOUSE-MOMENTS LATER

Pops is sitting alone on the porch. The sun is setting behind the mountains, the sky turning a dusky red. The playful vibe of a few moments ago is gone. Sonya is inside the house.

SONYA
(from inside the house)
He won't be mad. I bet he'll be
happy to hear from you. Late or
not.

POPS
He won't. The boy's just like
his mom.

Sonya pops her head out from behind the screen door.

SONYA
Invite him to dinner on Saturday.
Say it's for his birthday. Then
you can tell him about the
wedding.

POPS
I just got busy fixing up the
place for the wedding, you
know? It's not like I forgot on
purpose.

SONYA
You're stalling.

Sonya motions for him to call already and then disappears back inside the house. Pops SIGHS.

EXT. DESERT MOUNTAIN TRAIL-MAGIC HOUR

JD is farther down the trail. Beside him, running off in the brush, is a coyote. JD doesn't break stride as the thin, desert-brown animal keeps pace. The coyote's mouth is slightly open, exposing its teeth. Its tongue.

In the distance, on the ground and in the middle of the trail, are two blurry shapes. One is shadowy, appearing almost cloaked over the other.

JD's breathing slows down, as does his running. Now about ten feet away, the image becomes clear. The vulture from earlier is standing on top of the bloated, motionless body of another coyote. Its head is buried inside the coyote's guts.

JD stops cold. He turns to see where his running mate has gone, but that coyote has vanished. He again looks over to the vulture and the gruesome scene. His phone begins to VIBRATE, and from behind the thin mesh of his hoodie pocket, the IMAGE of Pops on his phone can be seen. The YIPS of the coyotes return.

The vulture pulls his head from the dead coyote's body and looks directly at JD. Its narrow face is slicked with blood. A worm of sinew dangles from its beak. The vulture's eyes are black and sharp, focused.

The VIBRATING stops, as do the YIPS. The desert is now eerily quiet. The sun is dipping quickly, the magic hour about to be lost to night.

Just then JD's running partner springs from the brush and toward the vulture, but the large bird is surprisingly quick. Its wings flap, and it soars away before the coyote can get close.

Then JD and the coyote lock eyes and freeze, as if neither JD nor the coyote wants to be the first to move. JD takes a step back and slowly turns away, starts to jog in the opposite direction. He looks over his shoulder after a few strides, but his old partner only watches, becoming smaller and smaller as JD picks up speed.

JD reaches for his phone and taps on the screen. He listens to his father's message.

POPS (V.O.)

Hey, Juan Diego. It's me. Your father. Sorry I didn't call on your birthday. You're probably all upset—I remember how you get. Listen, I called your má to see when you were coming to see her and she said you weren't. So I told her you were coming to surprise her. I made plans for me and you on Saturday at La Malinche. So you should see her tomorrow. You need to visit more and quit acting like a big shot.

JD is still running but starts to slow down.

JD

(out of breath)

What the fuck?

JD stops. He takes in his surroundings. A confused look spreads across his face, like a rat suddenly dropped into a new maze.

JD (CONT'D)

He didn't even say happy birthday.

CHAPTER THREE

DANNY GETS LOST, THEN FINDS OUT

It was easy to get turned around inside William Beaumont Army Medical Center—the identical corridors were set up like a maze—and of course, Danny was. He walked down one long hallway after another, each decorated with shiny military crests, flags, and bronze dedications to retired army nurses and docs.

It was his heart, Má had said when Danny called her after his meeting with Pablo. He'd heard raised voices in the background as she talked, a commotion centered on what to do about the Sarge. Apparently his father had fainted while brushing his teeth that morning, falling face-first into the bathroom sink and cutting himself below the eye on the running faucet. Danny pictured the blood washing down the drain. Thinning in the water and swirling away. *His heart?*

On the phone Má let loose with her own swirl of info. She'd explained how the Sarge had been born with a bicuspid aortic valve, which wasn't helped out by his high blood pressure or cholesterol. A normal aortic valve, she continued, had three small flaps that opened and closed, letting oxygen-rich blood flow from the heart to the aorta—to the rest of the body—and not leak back inside the heart, but the Sarge's valve only had two flaps. His leaky heart was a condition he'd inherited from his father, and he'd been monitoring it for years. Má's voice was matter-of-fact as she explained the details, almost like she expected Danny to know something had been wrong with his father's heart. But of course this was as shocking as the news of the Sarge fainting in the first place. Danny was almost running now. *Where the hell am I?*

Danny's phone buzzed in his pocket. *Má.*

Where are you?

Danny stopped in the middle of the hallway to respond—causing a trail of nurses and docs to quickly dance around to avoid bumping into him. Danny looked up, made eye contact with a doctor in green surgical scrubs and a white lab coat, her intense brown eyes glaring at him from behind squarish black glasses. Her hair, long and black, was pulled into a tight ponytail, whipping as she brushed by. Danny continued typing, telling Má that he was here, in the hospital. That he'd followed some nurses into the building through a side door and now couldn't figure out where the hell he was. Má responded to follow the signs to the ER—they were everywhere. Or find his cousin.

Má and the Sarge were always doing this—throwing him in some new situation, making it seem easy, and when he didn't get it right sending Roxanne to rescue him. She was his first friend when he moved to El Paso, her living with him and Má at Nana's for a few months. Roxanne helped Danny get his driver's license and was his standby tutor. Last year she had again lived with Danny, moving in before Juan died—while her parents were out of town—but staying afterward for months.

Near a bank of elevators, Danny finally saw a sign, arrows pointing left or right, toward the ICU and Radiology, or toward Cardiology and, finally, the ER. He spun right, toward the ER, his chest tight, his brain a swirl with talk about valves and blood pressure and inheriting hearts. He'd broken into a sweat. He needed to slow down. Breathe.

That's when he saw a picture of an old white dude in service dress. It hung by the elevators, just above the call buttons, rows of medals pinned to his chest and a serious *don't fuck with me* expression cemented on his face. The vibe of the hospital, with its flags and crests, the dedications and portraits, was, Danny realized, the vibe of the Sarge's office, that room a little military museum dedicated to Master Sergeant Daniel Villanueva. There were plaques and citations neatly spaced on the walls, awards his father had earned during his twenty-one-year army career, along with a picture of him in full service dress. There was a photo of Tata on the wall too, in *his* service dress. Tata had left the army after two years when his hitch, and his time at the war, was over. He'd died before Danny was born, but Danny still recognized the look on Tata's face, the expression exactly like the elevator general's. Like the Sarge's.

"Over here, dummy," someone hissed as Danny cruised by an open doorway. Danny stopped short, looked over his shoulder, and there she was, peeking out from the doorway, Roxanne, his pain-in-the-ass cousin. "What took you so long?"

"I came straight from school," Danny protested.

"Yeah, right," Roxanne said, joining Danny in the hallway. "You know how selfish you get. I bet you stopped for coffee first."

"And a muffin," Danny said. "Bad news makes me hungry."

Roxanne and Danny were the same age, and she'd been winning the better kid competition for years. In high school she'd been an athlete, captain of the soccer team. She'd also been playing piano and dancing folklórico since she was five and getting all As since six. She landed a full ride to UCLA—*a full ride*—not to mention a bucket of scholarship money from a fancy private college somewhere on the East Coast. To make it worse, she was both popular *and* genuinely nice. She was easily the shiniest penny of the family, even when she deferred the scholarship and enrolled at Community after graduation. Saying she wanted a break.

"I like how neither of us can ever tell if we're being sarcastic or not," Roxanne said, a sympathetic smile on her face as she hugged Danny, her arms wrapping tightly around him.

"Whatever." Danny exhaled, his arms pinned to his sides. He rested his head on her shoulder for a beat.

Danny had never bothered with sports and could not be credibly accused of being nice. He *had* been popular, but that was mostly because he threw wild-ass parties whenever his parents were out of town. Danny was more the pebble in the family shoe, which made him feel weird about going to a better school than Roxanne, even for a semester.

"Your mom and my mom are with the doctor now," Roxanne said, releasing Danny. "They told me to come find you."

"They always trust you with the most important jobs," Danny said, taking a step back so he could see her face before asking, "How's the Sarge? What did the doctor say?"

"Don't call your apá that. He's your dad, not just some dude."

"He likes it," Danny said, truth being his old man liked it from everyone but *him*.

"C'mon." Roxanne motioned for Danny to follow, moving in the direction Danny had just come from. "Let's go."

"That's the wrong way."

"They're moving him," Roxanne explained. She still hadn't answered his question, which meant the news must be bad. For all her badassness, Roxanne wasn't good with talking about the actual *bad*. Roxanne and Juan had started dating right before he died. It was gross how quickly they coupled up, how goofy-cute they were together. But he'd been glad for them. And then a cop took that away. Roxanne told Danny not to get mad but that she didn't want to talk about losing Juan with him, and it seemed to Danny like they'd lost two different people. Then Roxanne enrolled at Community part time the following year and started working at her parents' bakery—Fernandough's—like that had been her plan all along and never again mentioned her scholarships or the East Coast.

"What did the doctor say?" Danny called to her. "I'm not just gonna blindly follow you."

Roxanne whipped around. "I don't really know. She said it wasn't a heart attack."

"That's good," Danny said, feeling suddenly lighter, like a backpack full of bricks he'd had no idea he'd been carrying had slipped from his shoulders. He rushed to join his cousin, wrapped his arm around her shoulders, and pulled her close. "Right?"

"Right. But like I said, they're moving him. *To the ICU.* So something else is going on. They were whispering about it. Your má wants us to wait. She's gonna stay with him and text when we can come in."

"Oh," Danny said, the brick pack back on.

They sat in the hospital cafeteria, poking at their phones and sipping on coffee, little Styrofoam plates with picked-over muffins on them. They'd been sitting for hours, and Danny's mind had begun to wander, his immediate worry for the Sarge having settled into a slow-burning uneasiness. He and Roxanne had chitchatted about school, upcoming finals—she only had one. He told her about failing art class and his classroom outburst from that morning, about forgetting JD's birthday and inviting him to come over on the weekend—although that was probably off now. *Damn.*

"Only you, an actual good artist, could fail art." Roxanne was shaking her head in a blend of disbelief and disapproval. "I mean, you have to be putting in extra effort to fuck up like this."

"That's the only time I've ever been accused of putting in any effort at all," Danny said. "And I wasn't even trying."

"You're stupid." Roxanne laughed. She checked her phone, her screen lighting up.

"Who's texting?"

"My dad. I'm giving him updates." Tío Fernando was the

Sarge's little brother and a pretty awesome dude, in Danny's opinion. Did all the cool tío shit like sneak him beers at cookouts and didn't act all horrified when he found Danny smoking. Together Tío Fernando and Tía Carmen owned Fernandough's, a kind of modern Mexican bakery in Central. Má worked there too. Started when she moved her and Danny back to El Paso without the Sarge. So yeah, cool.

"Where is Tío?" Danny asked. A few months ago, Tío Fernando had let Danny update the mascot for his business, a happy little lump of dough wearing an apron, his face looking like Tío Fernando with owl-like glasses and a Pancho Villa mustache.

"At work," Roxanne said. "Why?"

"Because I like him?" Danny held his hands up defensively. "Take it easy."

But it was hard to take it easy in a hospital. The lighting was harsh. The air was stuffy. Noise was constant. Nurses and doctors came and went, grabbing quick cups of coffee and bottles of water. Premade sandwiches and salads. Fast-food burgers and dogs. The food service moved quickly, while everything else seemed to creep along. Danny felt like he was stuck in traffic, he and Roxanne inching along, destination unknown. Scary unknown.

Their phones buzzed at the same time.

He's in the ICU. You can come now.

The ICU was horseshoe shaped, the middle a bank of computer stations where doctors and nurses huddled, and along the outside were the hospital beds. There were no front doors to the rooms, only long thin curtains for privacy, which made sense. Why make it hard for docs and nurses to get to them? The Sarge was apparently behind one of these pulled curtains, asleep. Danny wanted to rush over and see him, but Dr. Rivera had stopped them at the ICU entrance.

Dr. Lilliam Rivera—the one who'd almost collided with him in the hall—talked as fast as she moved. She explained how she'd been running tests on the Sarge all morning and afternoon. *Putting him through his paces.* Danny held Má's hand and smiled at her, hoped to see her flash a hopeful grin back, but Má looked like she'd been put through paces of her own.

"Daniel has an aortic diameter of more than four point five centimeters," Dr. Rivera was saying. "We've known this and have been holding off, but he meets the criteria for an elective replacement of the ascending aorta. I think go for an aortic valve repair or replacement while we're in there."

"What does that mean, Doctor?" Danny asked, looking from the doc to his mom, then back again.

"As things stand, Daniel's dilatation of the ascending aorta comes with a lot of risk factors. We're talking dissection or rupture, both of which are major causes of morbidity and mortality. It's finally time. We need to do the surgery. We shouldn't wait too long."

"I still don't get what any of that means," Danny said, but not to Dr. Rivera. To Má.

"Parts of your dad's heart aren't working. They need to be fixed." Má looked stunned, eyes wide, mouth slightly open. Like she'd just been in a car accident and was unsure what to do next. Unsure how hurt she was.

Danny looked over at the curtain hiding the Sarge. "How long has it been like this? How come I didn't know anything about this?" Again to Má.

Tía Carmen and Roxanne hovered nearby. But despite that, despite the fact that Danny was still holding Má's hand, he somehow felt completely alone.

"Your father's heart has been broken like this for a long time. I think we were all so used to it being this way."

6

LA SIRENA

"Con los cantos de sirena, no te vayas a marear"

You hear them in the bedroom.

Mom and Dad, pretending to be quiet.

Arguing about you.

But the fight is not really about you.

Or at least not about what happened at school.

The white kid talked his shit at the start of lunch and by the end was crying, catching a straight right on the chin before going lights-out. You kicked him in the legs and back while he was on the ground. His head was next before a teacher scooped you up by the waist. You've had first days like this. In new schools. New towns.

"He can't go around fighting every jerk kid saying mean things. What are you trying to teach him?"

"To defend himself."

"He's gonna end up in jail, not college. We still gotta get him to high school."

"It's middle school. He's just being a boy."

"He's being a bully."

Mom says you need your familia, even if you don't know them. That you're alone too much and Dad should get out of the army. Your mom wants him to work with his brother, but your dad says Fernando borrows money from them all the time so what good would going home do? Your dad has plans for you. Your mom just needs to be patient. Mom says the plan should be *family*. And that your *family* is in El Paso.

"We need money."

"Not more than familia."

"They need money too."

"Money doesn't buy happiness."

"It buys bakeries. A house one day. A *future*."

"We're going. With or without you. *Now*."

Mom leaves the bedroom, the door wide open. Dad is alone, and you wonder if he is as afraid as you are, if he knows what to do after losing a fight.

31

LAS JARAS

"Las jaras del indo Adán, donde pagan dan"

"So you're not afraid of what's gonna happen?" Fernando said as he struggled to keep up with Daniel, his backpack stuffed with books, weighing him down. The walk to school was a half mile, and the brothers made it every morning, going down Raynor Street and past the Gonzalez house where Carlos used to live. Carlos had been a freshman at Austin High School—where Daniel would one day go—but he'd died in a car wreck last month. Daniel never knew anyone who'd died before. Didn't know how to explain the feeling of remembering Carlos inviting him to play ball at their neighbor Tungi's, always being nice to him, and then suddenly realizing that he was gone. And forever. Just like nothing.

"Apá said I wouldn't get in trouble," Daniel said, picking up the pace. "Not with him."

"I mean afraid of getting your ass beat." Fernando was now jogging to keep up with his older brother, to stay side by side. He had the confidence of someone older. "I would just lie if I were you. Tell Apá you did it and then forget all about it." Fernando waited for Daniel to say something, to acknowledge his good idea, but Daniel didn't reply. "I mean, I saw you and Apá yesterday. One boxing lesson ain't gonna make you a fighter."

The night before, right after dinner, Apá had taken Daniel into the backyard for a crash course. The sky had been pitch-black, the only light coming from the porch, moths banging against the bare bulb. Apá had grabbed Daniel by the shoulders and kicked at his feet, moving them shoulder distance apart, and explained that there would be no more running away from Adán Flores. No more getting pushed around. It was time to learn how to throw a punch.

Apá slid Daniel's right foot slightly behind him, bending his knees, and told him this stance would help him keep his balance so he wouldn't get knocked over with another shove. He explained that all his punching power would start with his feet and legs, then travel through his hips and end in the arms and hands. That making a fist was like grabbing on to a hammer—thumbs always on the outside and swinging like you mean it. Tomorrow, when Daniel showed Adán what was what, he needed to make sure that he didn't keep his arms at his sides or pop his chest out like some dumb chicken. Daniel's left hand needed to stay close to his face, to block, and his right was to drive straight into Adán's nose or jaw.

"Apá would know if I lied," Daniel said finally.

"How?" Fernando argued. "He don't pay no attention to us. He's always in the garage anyway."

"He's working," Daniel said, wanting to defend Apá and not sure why.

They cut through the alley after Lebanon Avenue like they always did. Dogs barked at them from their backyards, rushing toward the fences. They kept walking, not paying the mutts any attention. Most of the dogs were small and fat, them the favorite kind of pet of old ladies in the neighborhood.

"That one practice isn't gonna do it," Fernando insisted. "Adán really knows how to throw down. Dude can rain punches on you like a sky full of arrows, all aimed at your head."

At the end of the block a German shepherd leaned against the fence, her mouth open, tail wagging. Every morning Daniel and Fernando came to pet the old dog, the only one that never barked at them. The boys reached their hands through the chain-link and scratched her black and brown body, let her lick their hands as they patted her head. She was happy to see them, which always made Daniel happy.

"And what happens if I come home without a scratch?" Daniel asked. "He'll know I faked it. He'll probably kick my ass even worse."

"I can punch you in the eye," Fernando said, quickly pulling his arms back through the fence. Him ready to go. "It would be better than getting socked by Adán . . . or Apá."

Daniel imagined Fernando slugging him in the face. His brother's feet in the perfect position, energy traveling through his legs and swiveling through his hips and torso, his arms extending and an explosion of power at the end of his perfectly made fist, the force smashing him in the face. "I shouldn't have run away yesterday" was his answer. "And I for sure shouldn't have told Apá about it."

"Are you scared?" Fernando asked. "I mean, I would be."

"I don't get to be scared no more," Daniel said, knowing that's what he was supposed to say. Knowing that it was a lie.

CHAPTER FOUR
SANGRE POR SANGRE

"Ball don't lie!" JD yelled.

The shot rimmed out of the hoop, and JD snatched the board. He pushed the ball back downcourt, dribbling toward the old dude who'd called foul the previous play. The call was ticky-tack, JD barely glancing the dude on the forearm as he chucked a three that missed badly. He'd gotten up early that morning for work, but Raines had called and said to come in a 0800 instead of 0600, load barn canceled. The unit had a briefing with the chief, and Hermosillo wanted to talk to the crew right before. JD decided he needed a way to spend the nervous energy buzzing in him. Even though load barn was off, his trip to El Paso—and dinner with Pops—was still on.

"Yo," Luís called out, waving his arm. He was on JD's side, running alongside him, wide open. Luís always seemed to be on the court—at least when JD went—a true gym rat with beat-up sneakers and a cutoff T-shirt, sweat-stained bandanna. JD had gotten to know him between games, his story a lot like his own. Luís joined the air force right out of high school and did it for the college money, wanted to be a lawyer. He was the same age, a middle kid with an older brother and a younger sister. He worked as a fireman and lived in the dorm across from JD.

He was Mexican.

JD dribbled past midcourt, his eyes now fixed on the chucker trying to get back on D. This morning's open-gym crowd seemed older than the usual bunch. Slower for sure.

"Yo, bro," Luís was calling, huffing and puffing along the left wing, a clear path to the basket. Last year JD would've made the easy pass but not because it was the right play. He would have given up the ball—usually to Juan—because deep down he was afraid of getting beaten by a defender or, worse, stumbling over his own feet.

Now JD completely ignored Luís as he reached the free-throw line, picked up his dribble and leapt toward the basket. The old dude's eyes went wide as JD glided toward him. JD couldn't explain how he'd been changing over the past nine months. Since Juan died. Since joining the air force. It felt like a dead bolt was slowly being unlocked, a key turning and clicking inside his head. There were moments when JD felt zero fear. When he felt almost nothing at all. Now he effortlessly sailed by two other defenders, gracefully avoiding contact, and then smashed directly into the chucker's chest, violently dropping him before gently laying the ball in the basket.

"And one," JD added nonchalantly, landing over the guy he'd dropped. "And that's fucking game."

"Yeah it is," Luís said, breathing hard. "Pendejo."

A couple of the chucker's teammates were rushing over to help, looking incredulously at JD as they pulled the guy to his feet. JD and Luís were easily the youngest guys there. The only airmen. Open-gym hours were over, and the court began to clear. The chucker took a few tentative steps, his movements slow and ginger but seemingly okay.

"You're fine!" JD called out. "But if you can't keep up, you shouldn't be on the court. It's simple."

"Holy shit," Luís said, quickly turning away. "What the fuck are you doing?"

"Just talking a little shit," JD said. "Normal basketball stuff." The chucker studied the two airmen. JD could tell that he had something to say—*wanted* him to—but he kept quiet.

"These dudes are all chiefs!" Luís hissed. "They play, like, every Friday morning. And for some reason, you, a one-striper nobody, decided to run over one of the highest-enlisted dudes on the base *and then* talk a bunch of crazy-ass shit. You outside your mind?"

"Shit, I didn't know that," JD said, now turning away as well. Working mostly night shift, JD never really saw the bigwigs—they were all on days. JD hadn't even met *his* chief yet, the person in charge of all the people and planes. "Are they still looking over here?"

Luís glanced up. "Yup. But I can't tell if the vibe is disappointed dad or sangre por sangre." Luís put his arm around JD's shoulder and started walking in the opposite direction. "We should get out of here."

"Fuck me," JD said, following.

"Oh, he's probably going to," Luís said. "Like for sure."

• • •

Back in uniform, JD sat with Raines in Hermosillo's office, wondering what the hell was happening, why Rowe wasn't with them and instead outside in the ready room along with the rest of the AMU, waiting for the chief to come brief them in the hangar. The chief was Hermosillo's boss. Who was Rowe's boss. Who was *his* boss. Man, the air force had so many bosses. JD remembered meeting Hermosillo for the first time. He'd actually been psyched about it. The master sergeant had seemed like he could be familia. With his thick black mustache and matching, perfectly combed hair, he reminded JD of his tíos, most of them super vain and always acting like hard-asses for no good reason, which JD always thought was funny.

But after introducing himself, Hermosillo had pulled JD aside and explained that he wouldn't be getting any special treatment just because they were both *Hispanic*. That JD would have to earn his stripes the same way he did, on his own. JD hadn't known what to say to that, feeling as though he'd stepped foot inside an episode of the *Twilight Zone. You are about to enter a dimension where Mexicans become Hispanics and the idea of a brown person helping another brown person is a full-blown government conspiracy. Where like always, you are on your own.*

"I canceled your load barn this morning," Hermosillo said at last, more to Raines than to JD. He was sitting behind his desk, pecking away at his keyboard. Squinting at his two monitors. "The chief wants to talk to everyone about the deployment."

Deployment? JD forced himself not to look at Raines.

"Is our crew going?" Raines asked. "Because we failed the load yesterday. That has to be the only reason we went through it, to see if we were good to go."

Hermosillo dead-eyed Raines from behind his monitors, making JD fidgety as hell. Then they were dead-eyeing each other, as if daring the other to speak next. To avoid looking at them, JD turned to whack air force pictures hanging along the walls. Images of fighter jets blazing across the sky with the words DETERMINATION and AMBITION printed underneath. Pictures of Hermosillo and his family beside them. Him with smiling kids, two young boys. He was younger in the photos, slimmer. Happier looking. In the pictures he wore a wedding ring, but as he rubbed the palms of his hands across his face, waiting for Raines to break, the ring was gone.

"Still depends," Hermosillo said at last. "Do you think *he* can handle it?"

Hermosillo and Raines both turned to JD. Could *he* handle it? Rowe was the one who messed up the checklist. But more importantly: *Deployment? Where? When?* Danny's old man used to go all the time. He would ask the Sarge when he got to El Paso. He was glad Danny had invited him. That he would be staying over the weekend. But for sure he could handle it. No big deal.

"I think Rowe should be in here to answer that," Raines said cautiously. "It's his crew, right?"

"He wanted to talk to the chief about it. I want to see what you two think first," Hermosillo said.

"Well, what do you think, jefe?" JD said, stiffening in his seat.

"What did you call me?" Hermosillo said.

"*Jefe?*" JD said. "It's Hispanic for boss."

"Oh goddamn," Raines said. "Sanchez, stop talking."

"How long have you been in the unit, Sanchez?" Hermosillo asked, head tilted ever so slightly.

JD had only been in the shop for three months, which was like nothing. "You don't gotta worry about me. I don't care what Rowe says. I know what I'm doing."

Hermosillo raised an eyebrow. A small scar ran through it. "Does he?" he said to Raines.

"C'mon, boss. You know no one is worried about the kid fucking shit up."

BANG.

Hermosillo's door swung open. Rowe stood in the doorway. He didn't say a word, only motioned for them to follow him out.

The entire AMU stood in formation in the hangar, standing shoulder to shoulder in neat columns and rows. Rowe went in the back, arms crossed as he looked straight at the chief. JD, along with Raines, joined him as panic set in. He recognized the guy at the front of the room. The chucker. Chief Wilson. JD was so screwed.

Wilson was in midsentence, the briefing already in progress. ". . . Some of you have already heard rumors floating out on the line. And you've also been watching the news." Hermosillo came up beside JD, intently listening. "Well, those rumors are true. Our unit will be deploying in ten days."

JD thought instantly of the image he saw on the TV yesterday—of a mountain getting bombed.

"I was reminded this morning while playing basketball," Chief Wilson continued, "that if you get on the court, you better be able to keep up. So, let me remind you, if you wear this uniform, are in this unit, it's your job to keep up. It's your job to be ready for war. And in ten days we will be leaving to fight. And everyone standing here right now is going. No one is too close to getting out. No one is too young." Then Wilson seemed to look directly at JD. "It's that simple. Dismissed."

Everyone was stunned. The only sound was Wilson's boot on the hangar floor, and then the unit began a slow pour from the hangar, a buzz rising over with the news as they walked back toward the flight line, where the aircraft and the maintenance they still had to do waited.

Raines turned to Hermosillo. "So I guess that's that," he said. "Even though we failed—and by *we*, I mean Rowe—we're all going."

"Looks like it," Hermosillo said. He looked at JD. "Why don't you go ahead and take off. I know you're going to El Paso. Take a breather."

"Thanks," JD said, taking an actual deep breath, feeling the air expand in his chest. Wondering if he really could keep up.

CHAPTER FIVE

DANNY DRAWS THE SHORT STRAW, THEN PAINTS

"Breathe that in," Tío Fernando said, pulling a tray of empanadas from the oven. "Just take the time to appreciate that." He wafted the aroma of the freshly baked desserts into the air. Danny usually couldn't resist the smell, but he wasn't hungry. Not even for Tío's empanadas, which were the best in town. The smell of coffee also filled the air, which should have made everything perfect. But of course nothing was.

It was late Friday morning, and the house was nearly full. Tío Fernando, Tía Carmen, and Roxanne had stayed the night, Má spending hers at the hospital with the Sarge. They'd kept him to run more tests. The plan was to send him home before his surgery in a week—the earliest they could schedule it—but Danny wasn't sure Dr. Rivera wanted the Sarge to even leave the hospital. Her words kept turning over in his head. *Morbidity and mortality.* What the doc was saying was that the

Sarge had a disease and would die unless she fixed it. *We're talking dissection or rupture. Both.*

But the Sarge wasn't going to let her fix a thing without him coming home first. Danny knew the Sarge wasn't afraid of dying. It wasn't like his father ever told him that, but he talked about the future too much to actually be afraid. Anyway, Danny was sure the Sarge would rather die at home than in a hospital, especially if it meant he couldn't come home one last time.

"What kind are they?" Danny asked, pointing to the empanadas from where he stood by the sink. His uncle placed the tray on top of the stove, poured a cup of coffee and handed it to Danny. There was something calming about watching Tío bake. Roxanne sat at the island in the middle of the kitchen, also fixated on her father. He was a tornado of motion. Washing mixing bowls and stuffing them into the dishwasher, moving the empanadas to a cooling rack. He fired up a burner and placed a frying pan on it.

"Piña. Who wants huevos?"

"I'll take some," Roxanne said.

Tío Fernando cracked an egg into the pan; it started to sizzle. Danny sipped the coffee, the warm brew soothing. He'd hardly slept the night before. Worried about Má. The Sarge. His heart. Danny's stomach gurgled, and he gave in, reached for an empanada. "I can't resist these."

"I'll make you an egg too," Tío Fernando said. "And those empanadas are the only reason I'm still in business. That and all the help your father and mother always give me."

"Hey, don't forget Mom," Roxanne said. "And me."

"Of course not," Tío Fernando said. "Where would I be without my familia?"

Danny took a bite, the hot pineapple filling burning his mouth. He froze. *Is it possible to freeze while your head is melting?*

"Speaking of Mom," Roxanne said. "Where is she?" Danny tried to cool his mouth down with hot coffee, which was a terrible idea, his mouth now a molten disaster.

"At the hospital," Tío Fernando told her, taking the coffee from Danny and handing him a glass of milk. "Here you go, chacho."

Danny took a swig, then another bite from the empanada. The flaky, sweet but with a hint of salt, crust and fresh pineapple filling. Damn, they were deadly good. Tío was right. His recipes really did keep him in business. "Why did Tía Carmen go so early?" Danny asked. "How's the Sarge doing?"

Tío Fernando saluted at Danny and then gave one quick jostle of the frying pan, the egg elegantly flipping over. "Yes, sir. My brother is just being a hard-ass like usual. Your má needed backup." Tío Fernando slid the fried egg onto a plate and handed it to Danny. "Go sit with Rox. I'll get yours next, mija."

"Yeah, you're being weird. Even for you," Roxanne agreed, patting the seat next to her.

As Danny took the stool next to his cousin, he saw that Tío Fernando hadn't just made empanadas. He'd also hooked up a ton of pan dulce. Mexican wedding cookies. Conchas. Marranitos—his fave, them being cinnamon *and* pig shaped. All while Danny lay in bed not sleeping, Tío Fernando had gotten up early and was doing what he did best. Tío's being in the kitchen couldn't fix his father's heart, but his baking was doing *something*. And Danny could feel the medicine working. He felt better as he ate his egg and finished his empanada, not just full but cared for. Loved.

Three new Lotería art pieces. That's what *Danny* needed to do. He would finish them before the end of the semester, like Pablo wanted. In ten days. The cards were still in his room. Stuffed in a drawer. He hadn't looked at them since he'd finished La Muerte, the same day Fabi had given them to him. He'd finished Death quickly, but this time he would paint differently. Maybe not slowly but like the way Tío Fernando flipped eggs. The way he baked the best empanadas in the world. If Danny could figure out how.

"I see you drew the short straw," the Sarge said as Danny stood in the doorway entrance to his room, his backpack slung over his shoulder.

"Má said you gotta stay here at least one more night," Danny said. "But all your vitals and stuff gotta be good. And you can't be a dick. Then you can come home."

"Your má said I can't be a *dick*?" Sarge said. "That doesn't sound like her."

"I'm paraphrasing."

Danny hadn't actually seen his father since he'd fainted, only a quick *what's up* the night before while he and Má had been on the couch watching TV. What a difference a few days made. The Sarge's right eye was now swollen from where he'd hit the sink faucet, the stitches underneath looking like a small mutant caterpillar inching across. His hair was greasy and uncombed. He was unshaven too, white stubble poking from his face. His father hated looking like a mess, almost as much as he hated being stuck inside a hospital.

The Sarge was still in the ICU, which meant Dr. Rivera thought he wasn't out of the woods. Má had explained to Danny—and to Tío Fernando and Roxanne—when she and Tía Carmen had gotten home that the Sarge wanted to check himself out of the hospital. His plan was to manage his valve bullshit like he always had but with stronger meds. Basically, fuck surgery.

He wanted to come home.

Dr. Rivera had only been able to convince the Sarge to have the surgery after Má talked *her* into letting him come home *first*.

A TV was mounted to the wall, and a muted talking head blabbed on-screen as images of explosions over mountain ranges repeated, but the Sarge wasn't watching—and not just because his glasses were on the table beside him. Danny hated these news shows probably as much as he did. Má used to watch them religiously whenever the Sarge was deployed. Politicians and reporters, know-it-all experts, all talking about war like it was a sport. Like a game that would end nice and neat with winners and losers, with a score everyone could agree on until the next one.

"So, like I said, you got the short straw."

"I volunteered," Danny informed him. "I told them you'd get more rest ignoring me all night."

"I'm kinda sleepy already," the Sarge said, motioning for Danny to come all the way in. "But I'm glad you're here in person. I don't see you that much anymore. Ignoring your Instagram just isn't the same as doing it in person."

"You've always been stingy with the hearts," Danny said, trying to force a laugh. He took a seat beside the bed. The Sarge look suddenly wounded, and Danny wondered if he'd said the wrong thing. If heart was now a word he shouldn't say.

But then the Sarge laughed, too—a weak coughed-filled chuckle. He did look tired, his normally round face seeming flattened, his cheeks drooping, making his mouth appear small, his eyes sad. He and Danny were both quick to joke around, to say things they both knew were true but could easily be waved off. *I'm only serious* was the Sarge's favorite expression said in a light, breezy tone, his way of smoothing over a joke that cut too close to the bone.

"Damn," the Sarge said, catching his breath. "No punches pulled in the ICU."

"I'm only serious," Danny said, now smiling.

"Then I guess I'm in the F U," the Sarge replied quickly. He shifted in the narrow bed, his expression pained. His pillow had slid out from beneath his head, and the blanket around his legs was twisted. Danny jumped to his feet and pulled on the Sarge's blanket, unwrapping and smoothing it. He fixed his father's pillow. The Sarge shifted again, and Danny noticed how hard he was working to barely even move his body.

Danny went right to it. "Are you nervous?"

"About what?" The same blurry images from earlier, of an explosion, of dust and debris clouding into an almost night sky, repeated on the TV. The Sarge slowly reached for his glasses. Danny noticed that he winced as he put them on—must've forgotten about the gash underneath his eye. "About us going to war again?" he added, now that he could see. "That's somebody else's business now."

"About having heart surgery, Dad," Danny snipped. "You gotta be scared about that." They both stared at the TV, and Danny suddenly wondered what JD was doing. Shit, JD was supposed to come down for the weekend. Him spending the night at the house. Now he wondered if, like the Sarge back in the day, JD would be shipped out. He'd text him as soon as the Sarge fell asleep. Explain that he'd have to find a different place to crash and maybe wouldn't be able to see him at all.

"I used to be a nervous kid," the Sarge said out of the blue. "Now that you mention it. But my old man fixed that."

"Really?" Danny sat back down. "How'd he do that? Brain surgery?"

"You know what? Kind of." The Sarge coughed another laugh. He pulled off his glasses and again shifted uncomfortably. The Sarge really wanted to move, Danny could tell. To be on the go like always. He was not a lie-around type of guy. "It was the day I got my first concussion."

"Brain surgery and a traumatic brain injury aren't the same thing," Danny countered.

"Are you sure? Seems to me no one can ever figure out the brain, or the heart. Both just broken all the time no matter what anyone does." The Sarge looked into the distance, like he was remembering something from way back. "There used to be this kid who always messed with me. And one time, after I ran away from him, your abuelo made me fight him."

"And because you kicked that kid's ass, you don't get scared anymore?" Danny asked, ready to roll his eyes right out of his skull.

"Oh no," the Sarge said quickly. "I still get scared—I'm scared right now. But your abuelo taught me the most important part of being brave that day. Showing up."

Then the words sank in—*the Sarge was bullied*. He hardly ever talked about growing up. Usually he only wanted to spend time on the future, mostly Danny's. How he needed to get good grades. To work harder. To take things more seriously. *Fuck, to show up.*

"You've never mentioned a bully before."

The Sarge laughed again, wincing slightly as he did. "It's not my favorite story. But I'll tell you anyway. I mean, I'm only in slightly worse shape now than I was that day."

The room was dark, minus the light from the hallway glowing from beneath the closed door. Nurses flowed in and out to check on the Sarge on the hour, taking his vitals. Waking him up just to tell him to go back to sleep. They called him sir, or Sergeant Villanueva, and never asked Danny to leave even though visiting hours had long been over. Má had texted earlier, telling him she appreciated him staying all night. Danny sat crisscross on the chair, hunched over, sliding his stylus across the thick glass of his drawing tablet, painting furiously, nearly done. He'd been shuffling the Lotería cards. Placing four cards at a time on the Sarge's bed until he was practically blanketed. His father had long been asleep, his breaths deep and steady. Danny wanted to capture the vibe of the original Don Clemente Gallo cards, the bright colors and soft watercolor look, but he also wanted the otherworldly feel. He remembered what Fabi had said to him when she'd given him the cards: *The past never leaves you. In fact, the past happens over and over again.*

He was on a roll, doing quick flourishes of el gallo and el nopal. La palma, but, dammit, his phone kept vibrating. Pulling his attention away. Frustrated, Danny put his stylus down and looked at his messages.

It was JD:

Dude, I'm here.

Where you at?

WTF?

No! He'd forgotten to text him! Shit!

Danny looked to his father. Listened to the sound of his breathing. On the screen of his tablet, his new drawing glowed. This one more than a sketch and different from the original. Instead of a young man, the image was of a little boy standing boldly inside a soft blue backdrop, his back stiff and straight. The kid looked ready to fight, dressed in an open-collared pink shirt and blue pants. The number 12 sat in the top left corner. And instead of holding a blade in his hand, the boy clutched a pair of glasses. His face was different too, not blank and fearless but instead marked with a black eye, his mouth slightly open to reveal missing teeth. His eyes wet with tears.

El Valiente.

12

EL VALIENTE

"Por qué le corres cobarde, trayendo tan buen puñal"

"I can't see."

Dazed, Daniel tried to focus on a blurry Adán Flores hovering over him. A single punch had dropped Daniel, the impact like a light switch that had turned off in his brain and made everything in his body go dark. He'd fallen flat on his back, his glasses flying off toward the gravel of Señora Ramirez's front yard. Instead of rushing to his feet, or at the very least curling into a protective ball, Daniel reached hopelessly for his lost lenses. The kids who had circled tightly around Daniel and Adán began to back away, as if suddenly realizing the danger they were all in.

School was out, and like normal, Señora Ramirez had been both watering plants in her front garden and making sure the no-goods who went to the school stayed off her property. Her house was right behind the school, right across from the basketball courts where students, year after year, always seemed to gather and leave their trash. She rushed inside her house after seeing Daniel's head bounce against the sidewalk, her missing the part where Adán pounced on top of Daniel. Adán seemed like a haze, a very real ghost raining closed-fist bombs on Danny's head and face, on his chest and against his throat.

The night before, Apá had told Daniel: *Don't ever let yourself get pushed around. Tell that cabrón that you're a Villanueva. That he's a nobody.*

But Adán wasn't a nobody, and as Daniel took blow after blow, it became clear that the nobody was *him*. Daniel tasted blood, swallowed it as it oozed from somewhere in his mouth. He imagined what his head looked like, a jack-o'-lantern after being kicked down a flight of stairs, its triangle eyes and smiling mouth cracked and smooshed into a pile of goop.

"Stay with me. Don't leave," Daniel spat to his brother when Adán finally got off him.

But Fernando, the little fucker, was already running away. Him beating feet after Adán stood up, revealing Daniel's crumpled body and busted face, a pair of bloodied teeth punched out of his mouth and landing on the sidewalk, interrupting a line of ants. The circle of seventh graders booked too, as Señora Ramirez peeked her head out from her front door, yelling, "I called the police! On all of you!"

Adán took one more look at Daniel squirming on the ground, smiled, then stomped on his glasses as he ran off, cracking the lenses against the small rocks. Inching toward them, Daniel grabbed his spectacles anyway and put them on. They made everything appear splintered. As he tried to stand, falling back to the ground the first few tries, Daniel suddenly felt relieved to be alone. He'd always heard how misery loved company, how people could share pain. But as Daniel finally found his feet and started his slow, shaky walk home, he realized that was bullshit. Pain was the reason everyone had run away after the fight—even Adán. Everyone scared it could be contagious. Everything Daniel now felt—the pounding in his head, the sharp stabbing in his mouth, the sting of having to walk alone—belonged to him. This pain as personal as guilt.

CHAPTER SIX

EVERYBODY'S FOOL

JD's head ached, a stabbing pain throbbing just behind his eyes. He'd texted Pops, letting him know that he would see him that night. He thought about calling Amá, hoping to make it into El Paso before dark and see her like Pops had promised, but he craved sleep before the five-hour drive and instead crawled into his bed after the chief's briefing. The room was quiet and pitch-black when he drew the curtains closed. Even though JD had decorated it, the space still had the vibe of a hotel room. It wasn't so much the standard-issue wall locker or twin mattress. The plain brown carpet. The room had a temporary feel JD couldn't poster over, which sometimes made him wonder if he had a real home anymore. If he wasn't now some kind of nomad wandering whatever part of earth the air force wanted him to.

On that *actual* night, JD drifted off almost as soon as his head hit the pillow, but it wasn't long until he started to have the dream, the nightmare. It was always the same, or at least the ending was, and always jolted him awake and left him in a pool of sweat, mouth sore from grinding his teeth. Hands stiff from being balled into fists. The dream began at Danny's. JD and Juan parked in front of his elegant two-story on the east side of town, its ten-foot wrought-iron gate—intricate road runners neatly designed into them—and Spanish ceramic tile roof. The front yard perfectly manicured with desert landscaping, cactus, and trees in orderly rows.

They were in Fabi's piece-of-shit truck, the engine *put-putt*ing. The boys were silent before their road trip to Livingston, Texas. To death row. Where Juan was to meet his dad. In real life they'd been nervous, talking nonstop. Juan telling JD about the blog post he'd written in anticipation of the moment. JD blabbing about his documentary. In the dream JD knew what was about to happen and wanted to warn Juan. To drive anywhere but to that old building where Juan was going to die.

But he could not control the truck.

They blazed down the highway, zipping through traffic. JD tried to release the steering wheel, but his grip only got tighter, the wheel tossing him around the cabin. His hands ached. JD turned to Juan, who was looking out the passenger window. His face was ashen and pale, breathing labored and through his mouth. His chest heaving up and down.

JD had watched Juan get shot. Juan had been behind the apartment and JD inside the truck, waiting for Juan to ditch Fabi's gun and get back in. He remembered hearing the sound of the tires crunching the rock and dirt of the alleyway, a vehicle slowly creeping onto the scene. The cops surprised them both with their floodlights flashing on. The gunshots had knocked Juan backward, and the police quickly yanked JD out, tossed him to the ground. From underneath he could see Juan's body in the dirt. Still as a stone.

It was different in the dream. They were still parked in the back alley, the old brick building looming in front of them. The apartment's windows had been busted out, the yard choked with weeds and garbage, the surrounding rock wall completely collapsed. But instead of getting out, Juan remained inside the cabin of the truck with JD.

JD's hands were still stuck on the wheel. The engine running.

He struggled to get free, but it was no use. He looked over at Juan, who was breathing harder, no longer seeming to notice JD sitting beside him.

JD tried to speak. To tell his friend not to go anywhere, to stay inside the vehicle. But his mouth felt like it had been nailed shut. He grunted. The deep moaning sound came from inside his chest, but Juan didn't seem to hear it. Instead, his breathing got faster. Shorter. JD slammed on the truck's gas, but the vehicle didn't move. The engine revved.

JD stabbed at the gas pedal with his foot and wrenched the steering wheel left and right. Then did it again. And again. Nothing happened. Only the sound of tires cutting in gravel and the engine starting to knock. Juan was disappearing. His best friend thinning out like a cloud of smoke. Vanishing like a childhood memory.

JD was suddenly engulfed by white light, it bursting through the cabin of the truck. JD turned to Juan, but he was gone. And standing in the yard of the apartment building was a coyote. The animal looked right at JD, its honey-colored eyes fixed on him. Ears pointed and sharp.

JD's hands were finally free, and he yanked on the driver's-side handle, but the door wouldn't budge. He slid over to the passenger door and tried again. Both doors were jammed, and the windows wouldn't roll down. The knocking sound of the engine grew louder, faster. KNOCK. KNOCK. KNOCK.

Outside the coyote howled, the noise a desperate scream of high-pitched yips and barks. JD desperately kicked at the doors and the windows, cracking them. He looked over at the coyote. Now even the animal was gone. The truck's engine sounded ready to blow. KNOCK. KNOCK. KNOCK. KNOCK. KNOCK.

JD could hear the howling again. It was calling to him, but he can't figure out how to get out of the damn truck and follow. Where he even had to go. He shut his eyes, clenched his jaw. The sound of the engine pounded away in his head. KNOCK. KNOCK. KNOCK. KNOCK. KNOCK.

JD made good time to El Paso, feeling relaxed as he crossed the state line after clearing New Mexico. The more-than-three-hundred-mile trip almost done. There was something about seeing the familiar mountains and cutting through the crowded freeway that felt like home. At least in that moment. Felt good. But returning was also strange. While he was in Tucson, his parents' split, Juan's death had stayed in JD's rear-view mirror. But as he drove farther into town for the first time since he enlisted, and to Danny's place, he could feel everything from the past year moving in front.

He texted Danny as he made the exit.

Dude, I'm here.

JD was the worst at texting—or calling, just ask Amá—and was good for scrolling but never posting on any of his feeds or timelines. He should've followed up with Danny, made sure they were still good for the weekend. But why wouldn't they be, right? Danny'd have texted something.

Danny lived in a newish subdivision on the east side of town. It was fancy. Last year most of the houses hadn't been built yet, giving the neighborhood a postapocalyptic feel. This had felt especially true that time he and Juan had been chased through it by the cops, the ghetto bird buzzing overhead and busting up a party Danny had thrown only a few days after moving in. Lucky for JD he hadn't gotten caught. He'd have ended up in jail like Juan—probably wouldn't be in the air force if he had.

The houses were all finished now, the place almost completely unrecognizable. No wonder Danny didn't want to leave for college or move into the dorms. The homes on his street could be in magazines. JD thought so, anyway. He could see pools in most backyards, and some places had circular driveways, water fountains in the middle. Everyone's yard was immaculate. Not one with junky cars parked out front.

And almost every house seemed lit in some way, a warm glowing from behind shutters or open windows, from patios or walkway lights. Every place except for Danny's. Weird. As JD pulled into the driveway and parked, he looked the joint over. Not one light was on, Danny's car gone.

It was past ten o'clock. On a Friday night.

He wondered if the Sarge and Danny's má had gone to

bed already. But that wouldn't explain where Danny was—he always parked outside. JD texted him again.

Where you at?

He waited, shifting in his seat, looking behind him, trying to remember where he and Juan had been running that night, almost a year ago now. There was no sign of the dirt hills and wild desert they'd cut through, the landscape completely flattened and cleared. JD didn't belong in this neighborhood. Not then. Not now. His used Hyundai Accent stuck out like a Dollar Store in an inside mall. He'd picked his car up cheap on base from the Lemon Lot. The dudes on base were always clowning him about it, asking him if a wife and kids were standard options. He texted a final time.

WTF?

He waited. Still nothing. Not even the little dots, like Danny was thinking about sending him a message. Damn. All right, then. JD knew what he had to do instead. Call Amá. He pulled out of the driveway and headed toward Central.

Poor Amá had no idea he was coming—or worse, Pops told her he was going to surprise her earlier and he'd been a no-show. His old man always good for making things up, getting people's hopes up. He called Amá.

JD soon exited at Piedras St. The night Juan died they'd been racing down this same street, escaping a carload of gangsters wanting to jack them. He wondered where those motherfuckers were now. JD slowly cruised by his old childhood home—it was *sort* of on the way to Nana's. He stopped in front, noticing the new cars parked out there. A small truck with a rattle-can paint job and a pair of sun-faded two-doors. Blinds covered the windows of the house instead of Amá's thin curtains, slices of light cutting between tightly closed slats. *Damn.* Just last year JD'd been stressing about how he needed to escape this place, and now he wasn't even sure where his unit was going or for how long. He'd been too afraid to ask, not wanting to look too dumb. Too new. Too FNG.

A few blocks down, at Nana's, soft lights flickered from the front window. Her front yard was exactly the same as JD remembered it, the same neat grass and flower pots lining the porch, the nicho of La Virgen de Guadalupe beside the steps. The little brick enclosure looked freshly painted a sky blue, the statue of the Virgen nestled carefully inside. Nana lived near Austin High—JD's old school.

JD hesitated once standing on the porch, feeling nervous, like he was a door-to-door salesman and on the other side of the door wasn't his mom but a stranger pissed he was there in the first place. He knocked lightly on Nana's door and thought about driving all the way back to base. Because Amá had sounded irritated on the phone. *Yes*, he could come over. *Of course*, she'd been asleep. The door cracked open. Amá was in her robe, hair messy and in her face. Her eyes had dark circles underneath, and her lips looked thin, pale. JD should have just come earlier. Called sooner. He was the worst.

"I'm sorry for getting you out of bed," JD said.

"It's okay," Amá said, a small smile sneaking across her face. "Come in. I heated up some albondigas for you."

Okay, she looked a *little* glad to see him. And JD was surprisingly happy to see her, too. He'd missed her. And damn, albondigas sounded good. "Thanks, Amá. I haven't eaten all day." Amá and Tomás had moved in with Nana a month after he'd left for the air force, Amá no longer able to afford the house. Now that his father left them. Alma, his sister, now lived on the other side of town, in an apartment on the East Side with her novio.

JD followed Amá through the house, everything dark and in shadow until the kitchen, and sat at the little table, cluttered with plastic bowls, each one filled with onions or potatoes. Pinto beans. The albondigas *were* good. It was Nana's recipe, his favorite because she added extra meatballs with the carrots and potatoes, celery and cilantro with the soup. Her food was so much better than the chow hall plop he ate every day on base, a cafeteria-style spin on chicken tetrazzini or pot roast. Amá watched, chin on hand, elbow on table, as JD slurped down his first bowl and then served himself another.

"Why did your father promise you were coming today?" Amá asked at last. "What is going on?"

"I haven't talked to him," JD said. "He just left me a weird voicemail and hung up."

She gave him the same look she'd been giving him since he was Tomás's age, her face a mix of disappointment and irritation. "I know you didn't drive all the way here to actually surprise me or see your Nana. So you must be here to see your dad. Probably wants to celebrate the divorce being final."

"I don't know!" JD didn't want to mention the dinner was for his birthday—or could be; everything is hard to tell with his old man. "Pops doesn't talk about stuff like that with me."

Amá simply nodded, like JD had explained how the night

sky was dark and winter cold. "You know he still calls me," Amá said, rubbing her face. "He says he's sorry. That he feels ashamed. Can you believe that?" She looked out the kitchen window, at the old mesquite with the droopy branches that scraped against the glass when the wind blew. "He tells me that he still loves me."

"Maybe he does?" JD asked hesitantly, wondering why Má would still take his calls.

"Your father doesn't know how to really love another person." Amá's voice was flat. "Not more than himself." She kept her eyes focused outside the window, on the easy back and forth of the branches. "I should have known better. But I was a fool. I'm still that fool."

"You're not a fool," JD said, thinking maybe she was.

Amá took a deep, long breath. "He blamed me for *him* not being happy. Said I had changed. I don't think he ever even thought about me. If *I* was happy."

Amá stood up, her pain going from grief to anger, JD could nimbly see it happening. Her eyes narrowed as she looked at him sitting there, an empty bowl of soup in front of him. There was nothing JD could say. Nothing he could do.

"You know," Amá continued. "You should have stayed here with your family. Gotten a job and helped us." Tears started rolling down her cheeks. "But you flaked out, which I guess all you Sanchez men eventually do."

"Yeah, I read your letter," JD reminded her. "The one you sent while I was in boot camp." The one where she'd told him about all the moves happening. About him and Alma both being gone, a new family taking over their old house, and the only life she knew no longer existing. He'd been furious at Basic. *He'd* been the one abandoned. By Pops. By Juan—yes, by Juan. And Amá. Like it was *his* fault Pops had cheated.

"I'll send money," JD said. "I should've been doing that already. My bad."

"I don't want your money," Amá snapped, face pinched in anger.

"What Pops did was terrible," JD said, trying to keep his voice calm, "but *I* didn't do that. I didn't choose another family. I got left too. I've been running around the streets all alone for years with no one ever giving a shit about me. Including you." JD would never have talked like this nine months ago. He would have left the room. Brooded. Sulked.

"I was working," Amá retorted. "You needed things. You all did."

"Then let me pay you back," JD offered again. "We can be even."

"How did you get to be so mean?" Amá slowly sat down, slumping back in her seat. The way she was looking at him, was as if he were a stranger, an alien in a JD suit. He certainly felt different from the JD who'd left El Paso. Who did Amá think he was now? Who did he think he was?

"You know," JD continued. "You're real quick to say that I'm just like Dad, but really I'm exactly like you. Just as mean."

"Then there's no helping you, mijo," Amá said, reaching for the empty bowl. "Because then you're not just mean. You're a fool, too. A born fool."

CHAPTER SEVEN

DANNY SEES A SHOW, THEN HIS FATHER

The Sarge sat in the kitchen, going over Dr. Rivera's discharge instructions and trying to convince Má to let him have one of Tío Fernando's empanadas, but there was no fooling Má. He'd only been home a little over an hour, showering as soon as he walked in, saying he wanted to wash the sick away. His hair was still wet, uncombed, a soaked mop on his head. In just those few days he'd lost weight, the neck of his favorite Dallas Cowboys T-shirt fitting droopy and wide, revealing a protruding collarbone. Was that normal? Danny wondered. What wasn't normal was his father sitting at the kitchen island, a plate of apples Má cut for him in front of him. *Apples?* Danny, Tío Fernando, and Tía Carmen huddled by the stove, watching him from a distance.

"It says right here that I need to eat well." The Sarge playfully waved the papers at Má before stacking them beside the plate. "Eating empanadas *is* eating well. Right? I can still smell them. I know they are around here somewhere."

"Mi amor, you are always wrong," Má said gently. "You know that."

The Sarge raised an eyebrow at her in suspicion. "I've only been wrong once."

"And majorly wrong!" Má said, laughing. Danny was sure he knew the time Má was talking about—when she'd taken him and moved back to El Paso without the Sarge. Danny was surprised she was able to laugh about it.

"What else do your papers say to do?" Tía Carmen asked, moving quickly to the island and snatching up the instructions. "Lemme see. It says you should meditate. Do light exercises. See a therapist."

Now everyone was laughing.

The surgery was Friday. Dr. Rivera was going to replace the Sarge's ascending aorta *and* aortic valve at the same time, explained how each part was failing. Danny had never really thought about the heart that way before, how it actually *could* be broken in pieces.

"How about I just meditate as I eat pan dulce?" the Sarge tried. "I'll count my bites like they're breaths."

"N'hombre." Tío Fernando smirked. "I've seen you eat. There ain't shit mindful about that."

"Well, you guys are out of your minds if you think I'm eating like this for a week," Sarge said, pointing at the apple slices. "I'm not in kindergarten."

Only a week ago the Sarge had seemed indestructible, like a cactus that had been surviving for years under a brutal desert sun. Danny thought about the story his father told him last night, how he lost his front teeth, sent to fight a bully by Tata.

The Sarge had always been a hard-ass, constantly on Danny about school. About working harder. Reminding him about the sacrifices he'd made. But the Sarge had never once sacrificed Danny. Not like that.

"Danny will get them for me," Sarge said. "Won't you, mijo?"

"Say what?" Danny's eyes went wide. "Don't drag me into this."

"He doesn't know where they are anyway." Má laughed. "He was with you last night."

"So they *are* in the house," Sarge said, laughing as well. He leaned toward Má, scooped her toward him, wrapped his arms around her. Smiled big. "I'll find them."

"Good luck with that," Má said. "You still don't know where I hide your birthday present every year." She returned the Sarge's goofy grin with one of her own, and they kissed, hugged a long don't-you-ever-let-me-go type of squeeze.

"*Aww*, gross," Tío Fernando teased, him now scooping Tía Carmen up in an embrace. Planting a smooch on her.

"What is going on here?" Roxanne asked, joining them in the kitchen. "You send me to hide empanadas, which, by the way, is weird, and then this happens."

"All the grown-ups are suddenly in love," Danny said.

"They're just like us teens," Roxanne said. "But awkward."

Má looked at the Sarge, her eyes glassy. She was still smiling, but her grin wasn't anything like his, wide and a little wild. She was hiding, scared. The day Má said she was leaving, moving back to El Paso, Danny remembered how confused and afraid the Sarge had been, even in his uniform, which always made him look fearless. But now, even with him being skinny and frail, the Sarge seemed completely unafraid.

"I love you, Sandra," the Sarge said, hugging her again. And the Sarge saying that, the way he said it, like nothing he'd ever said was truer, scared the hell out of Danny.

Later, Danny escaped the kitchen and went upstairs. He wanted to get back to the Lotería cards. To figure out which he was going to do for his art class. He fired up his computer, got a new email ping:

> To: dvillanueva15@utep.edu
> From: pabloruiz39@utep.edu
> Subject: Checking in
> Danny,
> How is your father doing? How are you? I wanted to let you know we can talk about deadlines for your portfolio. Concentrate on your father's health. And your own.
> Also, if you're interested, I have some students in my MFA course who are showing work at Lincoln Park tonight. Come by if you are up for it.
> Pablo

> To: pabloruiz39@utep.edu
> From: dvillanueva15@utep.edu
> Re: Checking in

> Pablo,
> Thanks for that. He's out of the hospital
> but needs surgery. Can we talk next week?
> I appreciate the message. I'll see about the
> show later tonight.

The plan was to see JD later that night. *Maybe*. He'd seemed pissed—at least over text—about not being able to crash for the weekend. Danny didn't ask Má if JD could stay. She had bigger things to worry about, but yeah, he'd messed up by not letting JD know, putting him in a bad spot. He felt shitty, but like always, JD had his own family drama to deal with. JD was having dinner with his old man that evening and was supposed to text afterward. Danny closed his computer. Checking out the art at Lincoln Park would be a good way to help his own work. Plus, JD still hadn't made up his mind about going out or not. It was crazy how just last year JD had been an everyday part of his life. Then, after he'd joined the air force, they used to text *almost* every day. But that slowed down to a few times a week. Now they barely communicated at all. Just a few random *Yo*s. And *Sup*s. That was crazy too.

The columns towered over them. Danny asked Roxanne if she wanted to tag along, the two of them making the drive to Lincoln Park, a straight shot down Copia in Central, just a few blocks away from where Danny used to live with his nana when he'd first moved to El Paso. Not too far away from Fernandough's. Danny had driven by the overpass under the Spaghetti Bowl—a twist of highway exchanges—tons of times, seeing the bright colors of the mural at a distance, but had never gone to see them before. He wasn't sure why, especially as he drove past the ramp supports that cut through the park, curving with the shape of the road, each had a different, massive and intricately painted mural on it. One of La Virgen and another of Pancho Villa, of zoot suiters. Aztecs. The need to be close to them was suddenly overwhelming as he hurried to park.

"These are beautiful." Roxanne practically had to jog to keep up as Danny bounced from mural to mural. "I can't even believe this one." It was called *El Corazon De El Paso*, a red, fleshy heart dominating the column's center. Behind it were two Aztec temples transitioning into the Franklin Mountains, both cutting across a clear blue sky. A bald, orange sun beaming across. The other colors were just as vivid, bright purples and greens. Yellow and gold.

"They really are," Danny said. He felt minuscule standing there, and at first he thought it might be because of the highway itself. The constant roar of traffic whipping by overhead. The tons of concrete and asphalt, of steel, suspended above and around him. But that wasn't it. It was the murals that were imposing, *El Corazon* especially. Danny could not look away. "I can't believe I haven't checked this out before."

"No kidding."

Pablo's class was easy to find, set up by the picnic benches, next to a pillar with a mural of Dolores Huerta on it. The painting was like her famous photo, the black-and-white *Huelga* image except, now, her face and arms were bloodred, like the entire pillar. Dolores's giant body loomed over a crowd of striking workers in silhouette, a small SÍ SE PUEDE sign carried in the background.

Temporary walls had been erected between the pillars, and from them hung student work, a pop-up art gallery under the highway. There were folding chairs and tables with snacks and drinks on them.

"Should we go over there?" Roxanne asked.

Danny scanned the crowd, looking for Pablo. He didn't see him or recognize anyone from their class circling the art pieces. Did Pablo invite anyone else from their class, or was it all grad students? "I don't really want to—"

"Why not?" came a voice from behind.

Of course it was Pablo. He was dressed nicer than he did for class, wearing what passed for a suit for hipster types. A worn-out-looking blazer over a Chicano Batman T-shirt. A pair of dressy pants and his same scuzzy Chucks.

"Because he's nervous," Roxanne said to his teacher. "New people are scary. Plus, these murals are badass."

"I love these murals," Pablo said. "I always tell my students, anyone can make art anywhere. Then I bring them here to prove it."

"Okay, that checks out," Roxanne agreed.

"And who may you be?" Pablo asked.

"Danny's cousin," Roxanne said. "What's it to you?"

"And *that* checks out," Pablo said with a chuckle. "Come on over. At least come grab some food." He motioned for them to follow, heading toward the makeshift gallery. They followed.

• • •

On the walls were neatly framed watercolors, still lifes of desert landscapes. Woodcuts. Self-portraits. All the pieces were well detailed and crafted, with clear lines that drew Danny in. The artists' hearts were in each one, Danny could tell, but he couldn't help returning his attention back to the murals. These things were part destination, part road. Art that was much bigger than Danny thought art could really be.

Which had him itching to get back to his stylus, his tablet. "How long do you want to stay?" he side mouthed to Roxanne. "I wanna get back and get to work on some stuff."

"But we just got here!" Roxanne gestured toward the charcuterie board on the table alongside the open bottles of wine. "I haven't even tried one of these fancy cheeses or meats yet. Plus, you don't think your professor will get mad if you just leave?"

"I don't think so. I cussed him out in class the other day and then he invited me here. And if you're hungry, we can just grab some Lunchables on the way home. Because that's exactly whatever you called that stuff over there is."

Danny had to force himself not to speed as he drove home—okay, he sped a little. He'd painted on walls before, in his bedroom, only the Sarge had made him paint over them—the pieces from a comic book he'd wanted to write. But he'd never done a mural before. Now he wanted to check out different ones around town. Make a plan to go see more. He also planned to look up different artists. Check out different styles. Techniques.

When he got home, the Sarge was sitting alone, watching

TV. Eating an empanada, a flash of guilt crossing his face as he looked at Danny tiptoeing into the den. "Your cousin is bad at hiding stuff."

"I may have made them easier to find before I left." Danny took a seat beside his father.

"I knew you'd hook me up," the Sarge said, his face now a smile. The stitch caterpillar looking less pissed off under his eye. He was watching the news. Danny recognized the mountain from earlier.

"You watching that again?" Danny asked.

"I guess so." He took another bite.

"Why?"

The Sarge leaned back, squinting at the set, and seemed to think of what to say. His worry lines crinkled around his eyes and cheeks, and Danny noticed how his hair seemed more gray on the sides. As did the stubble on his chin. The Sarge suddenly looked much older. *When did that happen?*

New images of what looked like an empty downtown with abandoned buildings panned across the screen. The camera stopped on a bombed-out structure, the top floor of a three-story partly caved in and burning. There was no sound. Danny didn't know whether it was the video or if his dad had muted the TV, not wanting to hear the noise.

"How's school going?" Sarge said out of nowhere. "I'd rather talk about your classes than *this.*"

"I wouldn't," Danny said. They both looked back at the screen as a reporter appeared, talking rapid-fire into a microphone.

"School's important," the Sarge said.

"To you," Danny said, regret immediately gurgling in his stomach. "I mean, it's just sometimes I guess I want to do my own thing. Like you did."

The Sarge let out a little laugh. "I used to watch boxing with my Apá when I was a kid. And there was one fight where a trainer—he was the fighter's dad—pushed the son too far in this one fight. Made him keep throwing punches when he should've let him—"

"Quit?" Danny interrupted.

"No." Sarge chuckled. He reached into a ziplock bag stashed beside him and handed Danny an empanada. "There is no quitting. Not for you, anyway."

Of course there wasn't. Danny was certain his father had never quit shit in his life. He'd been a soldier almost forever. Married that long, too. "So what, then?"

The Sarge leaned back on the couch. "So you keep trying. You figure your shit out."

"So, just do what you want me to do, then?"

The Sarge's energy seemed to drain, his shoulders slumping, his head tilting downward like a toy suddenly running out of batteries. "Look." The Sarge sighed. "That guy's dad *picked* boxing for him to do. Trained him—and actually made him into a world-class fighter—but he should've let his son fight his own fights. My dad had been a soldier, too. And he *picked* the army for me, even picked my job. But I'm not doing that by wanting you to go to school. I'm not *picking* a job for you. That's for you to do."

Danny shoved a bite of empanada into his mouth. "I don't want to study economics. That was your idea."

Jolted with new energy, the Sarge scanned the room, as if looking for someone, *anyone*, to help him talk sense into Danny. "*That* was just a suggestion. Your tío runs a business and seems to like doing it. I thought you could do something like your uncle. You always seemed to wanna be more like him than me, anyway."

Danny quickly ate the final piece of empanada, not knowing what to say. He *had* always thought his tío was cooler. But of course that had shit to do with business. "The dude makes desserts, and you were never home."

There was a silence, Danny and the Sarge both trying hard not to look at each other. The Sarge stared at the blank TV screen. Danny suddenly focused on his tennis shoes.

Then, after a moment, Danny broke the awkward quiet. "How come Tío Fernando didn't end up in the army like you?"

"Because he had me looking after him after our father died."

"Oh."

The Sarge turned toward Danny. His eyes were puffy and red, swollen. He appeared worn down, tired in a way that was more than just sleepy. "Look, boxers make boxers, and soldiers make other soldiers. We know how to fight, and I didn't want that for you, to always feel like you had to be trading punches even if it meant you were destined to lose at the end."

16

LA BANDERA

"Verde blanco y colorado, la bandera del soldado"

The fight was on.

The rabbit ears of the small black-and-white TV poked at the night sky, picking up the broadcast from somewhere in Juárez. Daniel could hear the announcers talking about the fight, their voices full of adrenaline as they went on and on about punching power. Speed. Footwork. Daniel sat out in the backyard with Apá on a pair of metal folding chairs, the hinges and legs rusted from being kept outside. Apá nursed a Tecate, the rim crusted with salt and lime. Daniel had a Pepsi.

The once busted dining room table Apá had been working was finished. He'd replaced the old rectangular legs with elegant, curvy ones and carved smooth ridges along the edge of the tabletop. Then he restained the entire piece a deep cherry red. The table was drying in the garage, now something completely new and different, suddenly looking out of place in the junky backyard, like a gold coin that had mistakenly been dropped and forgotten inside a jar of pennies. The familiar chemical smell seeped out into the night air, mixing with the odor of cigarettes. Apá, himself always smelling like cut pine, lit up another frajo, a line of smoke twisting upward from the ash. He was ready for thunder meets lightning. The Great Mexican Champion versus The Kid. Julio César Chávez against Meldrick Taylor.

Apá had been talking about the fights for weeks—mostly at dinnertime and with Fernando, who now wanted *nothing* to do with boxing, with punching power or speed. With violence. *Chávez is Mexico,* Apá told them before heading outside. *For all the Mexicans no matter where they live. Like us, he takes whatever punishment is coming because it's for his family.*

Apá was glued to the TV, looking devastated as Taylor danced around Chávez in the early rounds, popping him with combos, looking crisp and smooth as he delivered that punishment. Daniel didn't know much about the sweet science, but he understood that what he was watching was some un-Mexican shit. Chávez chased and looked confused. Slow. Took big swings and missed, Taylor disappearing on him like a ghost. But Apá loved Julio César, loved the way he wasn't afraid to take a punch, because he knew the fighter planned on landing more of his own. *That's the Mexican way,* Apá kept saying. *Keep moving forward and always keep punching. No matter what. That's what being a Mexican, a man, really is.* The way Apá had said it was everything. His words like a prayer. A wish.

Above them the stars beamed bright, clear in the cloudless night, like they were begging to be wished on. But Daniel had already learned how starlight worked. That by the time anyone actually saw it, the shine was hundreds of years old. Mr. Ackerman had explained light-years in class, telling everyone that Polaris, the North Star, was six hundred and eighty light-years away. That one day Polaris would die, and they wouldn't even know it.

"That was a good one!" Daniel shouted as Chávez landed his left, finally cutting off the ring and trapping The Kid in the corner.

"Do you ever think about fighting that boy again?" Apá asked, keeping his eyes on the fight, not reacting at all to Chávez's hit, instead taking a finishing gulp of beer and tossing the empty. Cracking open another.

"No," Daniel said quickly, his tongue automatically running over his two front teeth. A dentist had replaced his knocked-out teeth, the new ones slightly whiter than the others. Daniel looked back up at the sky, avoiding his father's gaze, which was suddenly fixed on him instead of Chávez. He wondered if Apá knew about starlight. That, like his teeth, it wasn't what it seemed.

"At least you didn't let yourself," Apá said, looking back at the TV. Chávez was still losing the fight, but he was punching his way into a chance. "You stood up."

Daniel didn't tell Apá that he thought of fighting Adán all the time, just not on purpose. His brain randomly cooking the images in his head. Adán's fist striking his head and then finding himself on the ground. His glasses just out of reach. Fernando running away, getting smaller and smaller.

By the final round it seemed like The Kid had the fight in the bag, but he'd taken a lot of hits. Taylor's face was cut, swollen. And Chávez wouldn't stop moving forward, wouldn't stop punching. Apá sat on the edge of his seat, the ground around his chair littered with crushed cigarette butts and empty beer cans. With twenty-five seconds left in the final round, Chávez again trapped Taylor in the corner. He connected with a desperate, brutal right that stunningly dropped The Kid to the canvas.

"That's how you do it!" Apá yelled, jumping from his seat, looking at Daniel. "Pelea con todo tú corazón!"

But then Taylor staggered back to his feet, miraculously beating the standing eight. Apá's face suddenly changed, the joy draining from it as he realized what was coming. That losing was certain. But then, just as quickly as The Kid had found his feet, the ref rushed toward him and called the fight with two seconds left. Chávez, and Apá, had won.

Like Chávez's trainers and cornermen, Apá raised his arms with both relief and joy, as if he too had just gone the distance. Daniel kept his eyes on the TV, on The Kid, as his father then cracked open another beer, the can exploding foam as he quickly chugged it down. The announcer was saying that, for some reason, Taylor's trainer had told him to keep charging forward, to keep fighting that last round, when all he'd had to do was dance. And now Taylor stood almost motionless, his face busted and confused, his insides probably just as broken because he now found himself the loser.

"What a fight," Apá exclaimed, sucking down another beer and now looking toward the sky, shaking his head in disbelief. A grin spread across his face as he looked at the stars, like all his wishes had just come true. "That's why you never stop. If you always keep fighting, you'll never lose."

8

LA BOTELLA

"La herramienta del borracho"

The party seems like destiny.

Your dad is going out of town again. For work. *Again*. But Má is also leaving—visiting Arizona with your Tía Carmen. Both packed and ready to go.

The plan is to leave you alone. In a new house.

In the *new* house your dad has built, with three bedrooms and three bathrooms. Shiny new appliances. Wood floors.

This is exactly what your dad has been working for. Saving for. What everything has been about.

But already the home will be empty.

What was even the point?

Juan and JD are coming after their basketball game at your old high school. The party will be going by then. The kids from your new school will be there. You don't know them—not really—but you invited them anyway. You're sure they will come. A place to party is a place to party.

They will fill space.

Make sound.

No one has tried to make friends with you. To get to know you. You're a senior. An artist. You are alone.

Way back in seventh grade, Juan and JD sat next to you at lunch on your first day of school, both immediately asking questions: *Where did you come from? Why are you here? Do you play ball? Why did you sit at our table, which was cool, but why? Are you always so random?*

In this new house, as his parents left, your dad said to not mess anything up like you always do, which made Má mad.

They fight.

You get worried when they fight, remembering.

They fight as they walk out the door.

CHAPTER EIGHT

SCARED LITTLE BOY

JD could tell by the dumb look on Tomás's face that he thought there was no way he could lose a one-on-one. His little brother dribbled the ball between his legs as they walked down Memphis Avenue. He was only eleven, but the kid had handles. "You haven't seen my game in a long time, bro," Tomás bragged. "I'm really good."

"I didn't know you even played until this morning," JD said, swiping at the ball, missing.

"There's a lot you don't know since you moved away."

"Really?" JD sighed, irritation creeping into his voice. "Like what?"

"I know Amá thinks you ran away. She said you're a scared little boy. More scared than me."

"We'll see about that on the basketball court. And don't worry, I won't tell Amá how hard you cried after losing. You can stay her *brave* little guy."

Tomás shoved JD on the shoulder, barely moving him. "I'm not gonna fucking cry."

JD grinned at his little brother. "You're gonna be a goddamn puddle when I'm done with you."

It was early, the wintery Saturday morning cool. After JD's conversation with Amá the night before and a night sleeping on the couch, he somehow felt kind of…refreshed. The bed at Danny's would have been nicer for sure, but he got it. Danny finally texted back last night. The stuff going on with the Sarge sounded *bad.* He would call Danny later tonight, after his dinner with Pops. Hopefully everything with the Sarge would be cool and they could meet up.

It was JD's idea to walk to the gym. Get some fresh air. Hear the familiar sounds of music playing from the little houses in Central along the way. Smell food wafting from kitchens. Amá wanted him to take Tomás out and play ball. Spend some time with his brother. Apparently Tomás had gotten into it after JD left for Basic, started playing every day. Dribbling the ball in the house and driving her and Nana crazy. Amá said Tomás wanted to be like him, but JD wasn't so sure. His brother was probably bored, alone in the house, and found his basketball.

"Why didn't we drive in your new car? I saw you had a new car."

"It's not new. And I want to walk," JD said. "What's wrong with walking?"

"Looks new to me. And I walk all the time. I'm tired of walking."

Nana's house was closer to Austin High than JD's old house, just a few blocks up the street, but he used to feel the same way, tired of walking everywhere. To school. To church. The grocery store. It was probably why JD didn't believe in God or returning shopping carts to the little metal corral. "You're right. I'll take you for a ride later."

"Yeah, right."

"I said I'd take you. Relax."

"You'll be too busy, like always," Tomás said, pure *whatever bro* in his voice. "I heard you talking with Amá this morning. You're gonna hang out with Danny. *After* you eat with Dad. He's gonna bring his *girlfriend*, you know."

JD leaned over and tipped the basketball from Tomás's hand, sending it into the road. JD chased after it. They were crossing San Marcial, the street a straight shot to Juan's old apartment a few blocks down. "That doesn't mean I won't take you for a ride." JD palmed the ball. *Girlfriend?* Pops never mentioned any girlfriend coming. The dinner was supposed to be for his birthday.

And JD now felt an urge to walk by Juan's. It was out of the way, but the place always seemed to call out to him. In his dreams. Randomly in his thoughts. He dribbled the ball between his legs, showing off a bit for Tomás, and started down San Marcial, toward the apartment.

"Yo! That's the wrong way," Tomás complained. "You forget your way around already?"

JD reverse dribbled and passed the ball to his brother, veering back toward Austin High. He could swing by later. There would be time. Dinner. See Danny. A drive with Tomás. Stop by Juan's. He could make time before having to head back to Tucson. Before he had to get himself ready.

Deployment.

The thought hadn't crossed his mind—not really—since he'd rolled into town. He tried to remember what Chief Wilson had said. *In ten days we will be leaving to fight.* He looked at Tomás as he thrust the basketball down. The kid was thin, all limbs. His hair was long, in his face. Pops would never have let that slide back in the day.

"What do you mean Pops's girlfriend?" JD couldn't not ask.

"Yeah, duh. Dad has a girlfriend. It's the whole reason him and Mom are divorced now. Like, you're the one who figured it out, remember?"

As if JD could forget. Last Christmas Eve he'd been looking for tools in the cabin of the old man's truck when he'd found the condoms hidden under the seat. He and Juan later followed Pops, him and the woman leaving a bar and driving to her house in the Northeast. JD tried to remember what she looked like, but his mind was a blank, his head washed in booze that night.

They arrived at Austin High, and for the first time that morning, Tomás looked intimidated, seemed to be at a loss for words. The old, light brown building had seen better days. The paint was faded. The front lawn with splotches of dirt where grass used to be. But the Gothic design of the pillars at the school's entrance and the tower were still impressive.

"I know how to break into the gym," JD said. "We can play in there."

"Won't we get into trouble for that?"

"Nah. I do it all the time."

"No, you don't. At least not anymore."

Tomás was right. It was strange to no longer be a student. In fact, it felt altogether weird to no longer live in Central, or even in El Paso. JD had lived his entire life in this neighborhood. All eighteen years of it. But he was in the air force now. He lived in Arizona. He was nineteen.

"It'll be fine," JD said quickly, hoping to assure his brother. "We won't stay long. A quick game to eleven. On a gym floor, not busted up asphalt." JD hadn't shot hoops on a gym floor until he was in seventh grade, when him, Juan, and Danny all played ball on the same middle school team. He remembered how much quicker he felt, like he could jump higher, too. It was where he fell in love with the game.

"We should have drove. We could get away quick if we needed to." Tomás was worrying.

Ignoring him, and, like he'd done countless times, JD sneaked into the practice gym through the old fire escape. The door at the top was always unlocked, perpetually forgotten about. At first Tomás seemed freaked climbing the old metal stairs, wincing at the groans of the rusty steps. But he seemed impressed once inside, nodding his head in approval at JD, then dribbling toward the basket, shooting.

"Dude, this is awesome."

"Told you."

But JD didn't feel quite as comfortable as he used to once inside. The night Juan died, JD and Juan had been trespassing at the apartment. Juan and his mom had been evicted weeks before. They weren't supposed to be there.

Tomás was running coast to coast, shooting layups. The

sound of the bouncing ball was loud, echoing across the empty gym. Tomás was tall for his age but still had a little trouble heaving the ball all the way to the rim. What would happen if the cops came? Would they know he was only eleven? Would it matter? JD and his brother could be in real trouble, real fast.

"We gonna play the game or what?" Tomás said, stopping at midcourt. "I'm all warmed up."

Sweat began to slick down JD's back, like he'd been the one running the floor. "You were right. We can't play in here. Let's get out of here."

"What's wrong with you?" Tomás flung the ball to the ground.

"I don't go here anymore. You don't come here. I fucked up bringing you to this place."

"What?"

It was deathly silent inside the gym. JD scanned the windows above the front doors, thinking maybe he saw a shadow cross by one of them. He grabbed Tomás's arm and started pulling him toward the floor exit. "C'mon. Before the cops come."

But Tomás ripped his arm away. "Let go of me. I don't see any cops. What the hell is wrong with you?"

What the hell *was* wrong with him?

"I'll take you for that ride right now. We'll go wherever you want. Let's just get out of here, before it's too late." His heart was racing now, a hummingbird thrashing inside his chest, its long beak jabbing against his insides.

"Uh, JD? Maybe you should sit down," Tomás said. "You don't look too good."

"Yeah, for a sec." JD crumpled to the ground on his hands and knees. He took deep breaths, looked up at his brother. He needed to get him home. Out of this gym. This neighborhood. City.

"C'mon, Juan Diego. You're right. Let's go." Tomás tapped JD on the shoulder until he got back on his feet. JD felt dizzy but could stand. He nodded—*I'm good*—and slowly headed for the exit, Tomás keeping close. The door swung open, and the fresh air and bright light from outside hit them both. They were alone, but they still cut across the campus, picking up speed as JD started to feel better.

"Told you you should have brought the car."

"You're right," JD puffed. "We can still go for a ride right now."

"I'm hungry. Take me to a restaurant."

"You got it."

"But a good one. One that doesn't make you wait all day for your food."

"We can go to the fastest restaurant you want."

JUAN LAST CHANCE

ACT TWO

"THE DATE"

INT. MEXICAN RESTAURANT-NIGHT

POPS is sitting in a booth. At first he appears to be alone, eating chips and salsa. A trio of musicians, a SINGER, a GUITARIST, and a BASS

PLAYER are approaching his table. Pops looks upset, as it is revealed that Sonya is calling them over from the other side of the booth.

INT. JD'S CAR-NIGHT

JD pulls up to the restaurant. LA MALINCHE. He looks at the time on his phone, 8:35. He's late. He watches a couple walk by, them holding hands and canoodling as they move from the parking lot and toward the restaurant.

JD
(To himself)
He better not have his girlfriend with him.

He takes a deep breath and exits the vehicle.

INT. MEXICAN RESTAURANT-NIGHT

A SERVER stands at her booth, her chin resting in the palm of her hand, looking super bored. She appears to be the same age as JD. The waiting area is full of couples on dates and large groups of friends. It is NOISY.

JD ENTERS and immediately looks unsure of what to do, stands awkwardly in front of the server.

SERVER
How many?

JD
(Pointing at his chest)
Me?

SERVER
(Sighs)
Who else?

JD
I'm looking for my dad.

SERVER
(Like she's talking to a child)
And what does your daddy look
like, little guy?

There is scattered LAUGHTER. JD looks around and realizes people are looking and laughing at him, waiting for a response.

JD
He might be here with a woman.
So maybe like he's trying too
hard.

INT. MEXICAN RESTAURANT-CONTINUOUS
The server leads JD through the crowded restaurant. They stop at a booth where Pops and Sonya are waiting, listening to the TRIO as they wail away.

SERVER
(To Pops, loudly)
Don't worry, sir. I found your
son. He was very brave. But I
wouldn't let him wander around
by himself. He's just lucky I
found him.

Pops makes a confused face as the server smiles broadly—all cheese. She walks away but not before giving JD a quick smile and a wink.

JD watches her leave before turning his attention back to the booth. He looks at his dad, his plumber father who has disguised himself in a collared button-down and slacks, and then over at Sonya.

Sonya appears to be the exact opposite of Amá. Instead of a no-nonsense ponytail, hair pulled back tight, Sonya's hair is cut into a puffy updo. She has on bright red lipstick, and her eyeshadow is smoky, looks ready to steal a scene in some corny novela. She motions for JD to take the seat beside her.

INT. BIG-BOX HOME IMPROVEMENT STORE-NIGHT

Danny and Roxanne are pushing a cart down an aisle. The cart is filled with supplies. Drop cloths. Paintbrushes and rollers. A ladder.

ROXANNE

How do you know you can even paint on one of those highway things?

They turn a corner, and Danny stops in the paint aisle. Looks at the rows and rows of cans, at all his options.

DANNY

Oh, I got no idea.

He reaches for a quart of red paint. Examines it closely.

DANNY (CONT'D)

But I'm gonna do it. I'm painting a mural. I've decided.

INT. MEXICAN RESTAURANT-CONTINUOUS

JD sits beside Sonya. She is laughing, LOUDLY. JD's eyes are wide, looking super uncomfortable wedged next to her. Sonya, wearing way too many rings, her wrist bangled with bracelets, awkwardly reaches over and pinches JD's cheek.

SONYA

I can't believe how handsome you are. You look just like your papá.

She smiles broadly as she looks back at Pops.

SONYA (CONT'D)

If only I had a daughter.

POPS

That would be—

JD

Weird, Pops. That would be super-ass weird.

SINGER

(Interrupting, loudly)

Look at the happy family.

The trio is eager to perform another song. The guitarist gently PLUCKS at his guitar.

SINGER

What is the occasion? You look like you are celebrating.

POPS

It's my son's—

JD

It's my nothing. We're just
having dinner.

A frustrated look spreads across Pops's face, but Sonya reaches across the table and caresses his hand. She NODS at him.

POPS

(A little too loudly)

We are, in fact, celebrating.

SINGER

I knew it! What are we
celebrating, hermano?

SONYA

(Excitedly)

We're getting married!

JD

(To Pops)

You're getting *married!?* Are you
crazy?

The members of the trio look back and forth at each other, nodding knowingly, before they starts playing Carly Rae Jespen's "Call Me Maybe" in a distinct Mariachi style.

SINGER

(Loudly)

Hey, I just met you.

GUITARIST AND BASS PLAYER

(Together)

And this is crazy.

SINGER
But here's my number

GUITARIST AND BASS PLAYER
So call me, maybe.

SINGER
And all the other boys try to
chase me.

GUITARIST AND BASS PLAYER
But here's my number, so call me.

SINGER
Maybe.

The trio continues playing. The restaurant goers love the song, tables of people turning to watch the performance. The server walks another couple to an empty table. She smiles at JD and then points at the trio before giving an enthusiastic thumbs-up.

There is applause for the trio when they finish. Pops hesitates for a moment as the trio remains by their table, then reaches for his wallet and tips. He looks upset with them, and JD, but Sonya seems to have enjoyed the song, her smiling big.

POPS
(Smiling at Sonya)
When you know something is right,
mijo, you know.

SONYA
(Excitedly)

We want to invite you to the
wedding. It's next weekend.

JD
(To Pops)
Next weekend? But that's so fast.

POPS
Mi amor thinks it's important
that you come.

SONYA
(Excitedly)
I know this is so sudden, mijo.
But it would mean a lot to us.

JD looks incredulously from Sonya to Pops.

JD
(To Pops)
I gotta take a piss.

INT. MEXICAN RESTAURANT-CONTINUOUS

JD walks through the waiting area and sees the server, looking bored as ever, alone now that the crowd has thinned out. JD taps on his phone, sending a text message.

SERVER
I've never heard the mariachis
play *that* number before.

JD
(Still holding his phone)
I've never had dinner with my
old man's mistress before. Or I

guess now his fiancée. Firsts
for everyone!

SERVER
You know, I was getting pretty
bored with this job. But then
today happened.

JD's phone buzzes. JD looks irritated and glances at the screen. It's a message from Pops.

Text Message (Pops): Quit embarrassing yourself. Get back to the table.

JD
(Slips phone into his pocket)
What time do you get off work?
Maybe we can hang out? Talk
about mariachi cover songs as an
underexplored genre?

SERVER
No way. You look like you're in
high school.

JD
I only act like I'm in high
school.

The server studies JD, unable to hide her smile.

JD
I'm actually in the air force. I
promise, I'm all grown up.

SERVER
Be here in an hour. Don't be
late.

JD

I won't.

JD winks at her, then leaves the restaurant, not bothering to return to dinner with Pops and Sonya.

EXT. THE FOUNTAINS/OUTDOOR MALL-NIGHT

JD and the server, ISABELA MEJIA, are strolling along the elegantly lit shopping center. She is still dressed from work, a black polo shirt and matching pants. Her long black hair is twisted into a messy bun. String lights dangle from terraces, and palm trees twinkle from LEDs circling their trunks. JD and Isa are people watching in between sneaking glances at each other.

JD

So, how long have you been working at La Malinche?

ISA

Don't be boring. Ask me something better.

Isabel stops at a storefront, the sign NOTHING BUNDT CAKE above her head.

JD

Can you believe all these Mexicans love Bundt cake?

Isa looks inside the bakery. It is hopping with old Mexican dudes in cowboys hats flanked by their wives. They are waiting in line alongside young hipsters.

ISA

I've never heard anyone, much less my nana and tata, say, "Hey, let's go grab some Bundt cake."

JD

"And fuck it, let's drive all the way to the mall to get it."

ISA

And yet here they are, eating up all the Bundt cake.

Isa starts walking away, JD pauses for a moment, taking in the inside of the bakery before quickly following.

ISA

For some terrible reason, we always pretend to like things white people like. As if they'll be cool with us if we listen to enough true crime podcasts.

JD

That explains why I've been trying to get into Bitcoin.

They come to the Barnes & Noble. Teens are huddled around the entrance. Some are staring at their phones, others laughing and joking around.

ISA

(Suddenly excited)

Let's go in here.

INT. BOOKSTORE—CONTINUOUS

JD and Isa cruise the stacks, Isa stopping at a pair of chairs placed in the FICTION section and plopping down.

JD
Are we doing this for the whites too?

ISA
Books are for everyone.
And seriously, Bitcoin?

For the first time, JD and Isa are alone. He sits down beside her. Their arms are close to touching, resting on the side-by-side armrests.

JD
I was gonna be all about NFTs instead, but I don't fuck with blockchains.

Isabel laughs. Inches her arms ever so slightly closer to JD's.

ISA
I heard those are super dangerous.

JD
My cousin got all messed up by one. But like for reals. I wouldn't make that up.

JD and Isa are having a moment, them both leaning in toward each other, when JD's phone DINGS, causing Isa to back away slightly.

They again lean close, but JD's phone DINGS

again. Isa leans back and smiles at JD. They'd been having a moment, but it's gone now.

Defeated, JD slumps back and checks his phone. There are multiple unread texts messages, all from Pops.

Isa jumps to her feet and takes a book from the shelf in front of them. She pulls a pen from her purse and starts writing on the inside cover.

ISA
(Hands JD the book)
If you want to talk to me again, you're gonna have to buy this book.

Isa begins to move away from JD.

JD
(Standing)
Are you leaving? Why?

ISA
Not forever. Don't be so serious. Seems like you got things to do tonight. You should go do them.

JD
But I don't really want to.

ISA
And I didn't ever think I'd want to buy a Bundt cake, but here I am.

JD watched as Isa walked away, her strutting

down the aisle and then turning the corner to leave the bookstore. JD sat back down on the plush chair. He held the book, its corners sharp. The weight feeling perfect in his hand. *Winesburg Ohio*, by Sherwood Anderson.

Isa had written her number on the inside of the cover. JD rubbed his fingers across it, slightly smearing the ink. He quickly pulls his phone from his pocket and punches the number into his phone. He texts her:

Text Message: Hey! This is my number. Juan Diego Sanchez.

Text Reply: Jesus! Stalk much? LOL

Text Message: Not Jesus. Juan.

Text Reply: LOL

JD flipped through the book, stopping on a random passage. He read:

Dare to be strong and courageous. That is the road. Venture anything. Be brave enough to dare to be loved.

INT. BIG-BOX HOME IMPROVEMENT STORE-NIGHT

Danny and Roxanne stand in line at the register. The cart is now completely full of supplies, cans of paint piled on top. A CASHIER is ringing them up.

ROXANNE

How you gonna pay for all this?

DANNY

Pops's credit card. He said I could use it for school.

Roxanne raised a suspicious eyebrow at her cousin.

ROXANNE

And this is for school? Really?

DANNY

Pablo said I need to do three new paintings to pass the semester. So, I gotta do three murals. I'm gonna need a lot of shit.

Danny shrugged as the cashier kept ringing up the supplies. The total going higher and higher.

ROXANNE

(Mumbling to herself)

You're gonna *be* in a lotta shit.

EXT. NANA'S HOUSE/PORCH-NIGHT

A shadowy figure stands on the dimly lit porch, smoking a cigarette and watching as JD's car drives up the street and pulls into the driveway. Thick plumes of cigarette smoke cloud the air.

JD hesitates inside his car for a beat, trying to see who the person on the porch is.

It's Pops.

CUT TO:

JD looks upset standing on the opposite side of the porch. Pops just appears tired. He takes a drag from his cigarette and begins to pace. JD studies him as he moves back and forth.

NOISES come from inside the house. It is mostly dark inside, save for the kitchen where a sole light was on. Amá is in there. Probably putting dinner dishes away. Probably trying to listen.

JD

Did you say hi to Amá?

Pops stops pacing. Eyeballs JD.

POPS

What do you think?

JD

I don't know. You're all surprises.

POPS

Of course I said hello. I also told her how you ran off during dinner like a little brat . . . She laughed.

JD laughs too.

JD

Good.

POPS

(Chuckling)

It's not funny.

JD
Did you tell her you're getting married next week? Did you invite her too?

Pops turns serious again, looks out into the neighborhood. His back to JD—JD is frustrating the shit out of him.

POPS
(Takes a deep breath)
I told her I wanted you to come to it. That I wanted my son there.

JD
I bet she liked that.

POPS
You know, I remember picking your amá up for our first date on this porch. I parked where you're parked now. Came up these same steps.

The kitchen light is still on in the house, but there is no sign of Amá. From the porch we can see a section of the kitchen table and stove, a baker's rack with plastic containers of flour and sugar, maizena.

There is a distant photograph hanging just in frame above the stove. As Pops continues to speak, the camera zooms in on the image.

POPS (OS)
She wanted to go to Western Playland, which I didn't wanna do. Roller coasters weren't

really my thing, but I went with
it. I had a good time going on
all the rides. Eating ice cream.

The image is of a young Amá. She is smiling wide, holding the hand of a Young Girl and carrying a Baby, JD.

POPS (OS) (CONT'D)
I fell in love with your mom
pretty fast. We got married after
dating a year. Things were good
starting off. We had fun. But
she wanted kids, a family. And
we did that fast too. Everything
we did was fast.

JD (OS)
This story ain't fast.

The camera focuses on the Young Girl and then the Baby as Pops continues his story.

POPS (OS)
(Ignoring JD)
When you do make decisions
too quickly, without thinking,
your life gets away from you.
The person you love, the one
whipping around with you on
a roller coaster changes into
somebody else. Or maybe they
were always somebody else and
you never noticed. Eventually
life slowed down, and I realized
I wasn't happy. I realized I'd
made a mistake getting married
too young.

The image of young Amá could not look happier as Pops is talking, her face beaming. Then the light suddenly cuts out. Blackness.

POPS

I still love your Amá, mijo. Because of you kids. But I love Sonya now.

There is a moment of quiet. Pops turns and faces JD. He turns out his cigarette, as if preparing for an embrace. Maybe a fight. JD looks back inside Nana's, everything now completely dark. Silent.

JD

All that sounds like a bullshit way to say you had kids, got bored, and started chasing pussy. Fuck off, Dad.

JD rushes by Pops and from the porch, leaving his father gobsmacked. Pops looks around, as if for a witness to what JD has just said.

JD jumps into his car, the headlights flipping on. The engine comes to life and he drives away.

INT./EXT. JD'S CAR/EL PASO/NEIGHBORHOOD-LATER

JD is driving. The sound of beer bottles CLINKING together can be heard in the cabin. JD pulls up to a four-way stop. He is at the corner of Memphis and Altura Avenue. Sitting underneath the stop sign is a coyote. *Can it be the same one? From my run the other day?*

JD

What the fuck?

He takes a pull from a 40, revealing that he's been drinking. He lowers his driver's-side window and leans his head out.

Outside the coyote tilts his head, ears perked, hearing the mechanical noise. The animal watches JD.

YIPS and HOWLS call out, and the coyote turns and follows the noises, running down Altura Avenue. JD hesitates for a beat before following.

He drives slowly, keeping behind the coyote as it runs down the side of the road before darting off between a pair of houses, and JD stops.

He has arrived at Juan's old home, his headlights lighting up the abandoned building.

CHAPTER NINE
DANNY MAKES A PLAN

Killing the headlights, Danny let the engine run for a spell. He stopped in the usual spot, where he'd parked countless times when he'd come to hang with Juan and JD.

Meet me at Juan's, the first message read.

Then, **Yo! I'm here.**

Followed by, **It's important. Hurry up.**

Then finally, **where the fuck R U?**

It had never crossed Danny's mind to not meet after JD's first text, but as he sat in the alleyway at the back of the abandoned apartment building, he wondered why it hadn't. Not only was it late and his car full of painting supplies, but the very idea of being where Juan died seemed worse and worse the more he thought about it. *Why ever come back here?*

He looked around. The place was a wreck. Well, it had always been a wreck, but now it had really gone to shit. Weeds had choked out the backyard, waist high and now turned yellow, the spiky arms curling up, ready to break free from the hard ground and tumble away. Juan's old building, the tallest in the neighborhood, was worse off than the yard. The windows had been busted out. Some were covered with plywood, others just gaping black holes behind remaining shards of glass. The walls were tagged with scrawls of spray paint. The neighboring houses, on the other hand, still looked like they always did. Nothing fancy about the old brick homes, but still lived in.

Then, holy shit—he noticed that the wall in the back of the property had collapsed. He cut the engine, remembered how he, Juan, and JD used to hop over it after school and sit on milk crates in the backyard and smoke. In the far corner of the yard where they pounded 40s and bullshitted for hours, no one in the apartment complex ever going back there, the space all their own. The toolshed where they'd kept the milk crates was gone now. As was the cheap patio furniture that junked up the small back porch. The entire scene seemed as dead as Juan.

Where the hell is JD? Danny looked around, uneasily this time, and saw the back door had been kicked open, the wooden frame splintered, the door half off its hinges and with a hole cratered in it. Danny thought about texting JD, even though he already knew where he was. Inside the building. Such a bad idea. They were already trespassing just being in the yard, but actually *breaking and entering* was way worse. For sure it was a bigger crime, but also, the notion of poking around in Juan's old place seemed like some kind of an invasion, not just of Juan's home but his private life. Danny had loved hanging at Juan's—almost all his memories there good ones—but snooping around could easily paint over them, glimpses into Juan's private life like a coat of white semi-gloss rolling over the colorful and intricate mural of Danny's memories, leaving them both visible but unrecognizable underneath. Still, he hopped out of the car.

"Hey," Danny called out hesitantly from the back porch. "Is your dumbass in there?" He peeked his head inside, using the flashlight on his phone to see the collection of empty beer bottles and cans pocketed along the narrow hallway. Danny imagined the kids who partied there, probably students at Austin High looking for a private place to hang, maybe one or two having lived in the building and telling their friends about it. Aside from the trash, the place didn't look too beat-up—at least not any more than it had before. Yeah, the windows had been busted, the back door kicked in, but inside the walls were intact, no holes or anything. The light fixtures along the hallway were covered in spiderwebs but not ripped from the walls. The battle of vandalism versus decay looking like a tie.

"Why the fuck you yelling?" It was JD, also yelling. His head popped out from the door—Juan's door—at the end of the hallway. "Last time the cops came here, shit didn't go so good."

"Really?" Danny played along. "What happened?" He stepped lightly as he continued down the hallway, just like he used to when visiting Juan. Not wanting to clomp around and disturb the closed doors on either side of him—Juan's neighbors.

"You don't remember," JD deadpanned. "They murdered Juan."

"Is that where he's been?" Danny said. "I guess that's a good excuse for ignoring my texts. What's yours?"

JD glared at Danny, his face as blank as a brick wall. "You're a fucking needy," he said, finally cracking a smile and wildly motioning for Danny to follow him. But at Juan's door, the last one at the end of the narrow corridor, Danny found himself hesitating. He could hear Pablo's words echoing in his head. *A hallway can be anything.*

He forced himself forward through the open door and into the empty living room. The room was smaller than he remembered, the walls stained and bare, a tangled extension cord and small trash can—filled with crumpled papers—the only things inside. Danny remembered where the mismatched sofas had been, the TV where they'd watched basketball. The old carpet was worn, the concrete slab underneath beginning to show in spots. Juan's bedroom was just as empty as the living room, though his old window now had a gaping hole in it, a rock and shards of glass sprinkled on the floor in front of it. The entire apartment was like a broken shell, Danny thought. Whatever life had once been housed inside having crawled away a long time ago.

"What are we even doing here?" Danny turned to JD. "This feels fucked up." He knew the bedroom wasn't Juan's anymore, but still, he felt like an intruder. Like he was about to read Juan's diary or something.

JD plopped down beside the busted window, a gust of cold wind blowing through it, making a whistling sound. JD *was* drunk AF. He took a pull from a 40, and as he drank, the image of the Lotería card, El Borracho, suddenly appeared in Danny's head. In the original the old drunk was outside a shuttered building, him about to tumble over on a yellow bricked sidewalk, his clothes ripped up.

"I followed a coyote here."

"What?" Danny moved back from the window. "I thought you weren't allowed to do mushrooms in the air force." Danny's version of El Borracho would be set in a room just like this, he decided. The borracho young, his face on the verge of tears and sitting defeated beside a busted window. The wall behind him would be bare, minus the tiny holes and shadowed outlines where picture frames used to be. When JD didn't answer, he added, "So, I'm guessing your dinner went like shit."

JD rested the back of his head against the wall, looking intently at the 40 in his hand. The top of the bottle smudged with his fingerprints. "Two stars. The service was slow, and the only thing on the menu was my dad getting married to his mistress. Next Saturday."

"Sounds like a one star," Danny said.

"Restaurant had a cool band," JD said, then after a bit, "My old man just sucks."

"Mine was just in the hospital," Danny said. "Almost died, but I told you that already."

JD suddenly looked ready to cry. He seemed to be apologizing, though Danny wasn't sure for what. Both he and JD liked to talk a lot of crap. Probably too much.

Danny slumped down beside JD. He was realizing how Juan had been the one who kept things real between the three of them. Maybe that was why they'd both come here. For some kind of truth. "Yo. I'm sorry your dad sucks."

JD rolled his neck. "He just won't stop being the same guy he's always been."

"Why can't people just stop being themselves, like for once?" Danny added. Why couldn't *he* stop? He wondered if it would always be this way for him and JD. If, like Pops, like the Sarge, they were doomed to always be the same.

"For reals." JD side-eyed Danny. He continued. "I know I'm being a stupid baby, right. I just thought that after last year, everything wouldn't still be terrible." JD turned his attention to a stain on the carpet in front of him. The dark splotch looked like a hole, round and black. Big enough for both of them to fall into. "I think I made a huge mistake joining the air force. I joined too fast, without thinking about it."

"Nah. Your big mistake is being a stupid baby," Danny said. "Have you tried *not* being a stupid baby?"

"Can people do that?" JD asked, eyes glassy and red.

"Of course not," Danny said. "People are what they are."

"So I guess we're fucked," JD said.

They laughed, then sat in silence, both drifting off into their own worlds. Danny thought about the Sarge. His father *was* always the same guy, but Danny knew he would miss him if one day he wasn't. If he was gone. Was *that* fucked? "I should get home," he said.

JD pressed his hand into the carpet, pushing himself up as tiny shards of broken glass dug into his palm. Wincing, he studied the little drops of blood beginning to form. "I don't think I gotta real home anymore."

Danny hopped up, leaned in to study the shards of glass

poking up from JD's hand. "I thought you military guys ended up homeless *after* getting out?"

"I'm pretty advanced," JD said. "I'm ahead on my drinking problem too."

"Brag." Danny wanted to keep laughing but didn't know if JD was trying to be funny or not. The Sarge had bounced from place to place early in his army days, and Danny wondered if his father had felt the same way. Like he didn't belong anywhere.

JD picked a piece of glass from his hand. Studied the shard, blood staining the fractured glass red. "What I mean is that I have a room I live in but not like a home, home. It's hard to explain."

"I know shit was fucked up this weekend because my dad was in the hospital," Danny said. "But you can always crash with me, man. We're boys. No matter what."

JD picked a final bloodied piece of glass from his palm, flicked it back onto the floor. He wiped his palm on his hoodie, smearing a deep red stain across the gray. "I don't know what to say to that," JD said. "Thanks, I guess."

"You guess?" Danny gasped, incredulous. "How about you eat shit?"

They laughed. A happy grin eased on JD's face. "It almost feels like the old times," JD observed. "Us talking crazy. All we need is Juan."

"Except Juan would always stop us so he could talk about basketball and whatever the fuck he was gonna do way off in the future," Danny said.

The smile on JD's face vanished. "Yeah, that fool always

had a plan. He even got me thinking that way. I sometimes feel like I fucked up joining the air force to make movies, because I definitely ain't making movies."

"So, start making one. I don't know why you just don't go for it." Danny waved his hand to where the TV used to be. "Get on YouTube and figure it out."

"Last time I just tried to make a movie, Juan died," JD said flatly.

"Yeah, that's what killed him. Bad camera angles and sound."

JD moved farther away from Danny, legs unsteady as he stood in the middle of the room. "Watching YouTube isn't going to college, bro. Putting up stuff for clicks and likes isn't directing a film." JD sounded defensive, angry. He looked Danny in the eyes. "No one's helping me. I didn't have some teacher or coach who had my back. Parents who could hook me up. You know, Juan always thought you talked too much crap about your old man. Maybe he's some kind of asshole, but you have one. All the dude wants is for you to not suck."

Danny turned away, looked out the broken window, at his car parked in the alleyway. That wasn't exactly right. Danny never remembered talking *that much crap*. And seriously? The Sarge could be *hard*, treating him more like a private than his son. Danny wanted to go the hell home, but no way could he leave JD here all alone. He was too messed up, in too many ways. So, "Let me drive you home," is how he responded.

"I can drive. My car's up front, next to the tagged-up for-sale sign." JD gave a short laugh. "Like anyone would ever wanna buy this place?"

"That's your Hyundai?" Danny smirked, sidestepping the

driving topic. "I thought some soccer mom broke down and just abandoned her ride."

"Whatever." JD glanced out the window, rubbed his face, smearing specs of blood across it from his cut hand. What a mess. "But to be honest, seeing the backyard again kinda fucked me up. I mean, just looking at it now . . ." JD trailed off.

"I get it," Danny said, even though he didn't, not really. He wasn't there that night, didn't see his best friend killed the way JD had. He was sure JD was in the air force for the college money, but it suddenly dawned on him that what had happened to him that night had pushed him there. He put his arm around JD's shoulder, an idea forming. "C'mon, let's go."

"Where we going?" JD asked, unsteadily following Danny down the hallway.

They cut quickly through the backyard toward Danny's car, standing side by side as they reached the passenger door, neither saying anything. Until Danny finally did.

"I wanna clean this place up," Danny said. "Rip out the weeds. Pick up all the trash. Let's do that. We can start tomorrow. I'll get my cousin to help. For Juan."

"What? *Why?*"

"It shouldn't be like this," Danny answered.

"Another slum lord is gonna eventually buy this place, slap a cheap coat of paint on it and rent out rooms to motherfuckers who can't afford any better. The next Juan who lives here will have no idea that another Juan just like him used to live here. And no Juan will remember shit about what happened."

Danny unlocked the doors to his car, the headlights flashing and the locks making their thunking sound. His plastic bags of painting supplies visible in the back seat. "Are you proud of those puns?"

"Just the first Juan," JD said, chin raised.

But what if that's not all they did? Danny's brain was buzzing now, seeing his paint supplies. What if instead of a cheap coat of paint, the walls were covered with murals? Danny imagined El Borracho. It beside El Valiente. And La Muerte. He studied the back of the building. For sure four Lotería cards would fit. Maybe more. They could clean up the backyard, nail plywood over the busted windows. Forget the columns of Lincoln Park. He would paint his murals *here*. At Juan's.

"So, you gonna help me clean up?" Danny was pumped. "Because I got another favor to ask."

JD stumbled back a bit, blinking. Clearly not understanding the question. "What's the second favor?"

"I want to paint a mural on the building. I could use your help with that, too."

"Nah." JD turned to look behind him. He'd been staring out into the neighborhood, his attention somewhere else but ignoring Danny. Danny could tell JD was somehow different, the military having changed him. And it wasn't just his fade, which was a little higher, a little tighter. He stood straighter—even while completely trashed—and he talked that way too. "I'll help you clean it up, but I don't think you should paint anything. Juan died right there." He pointed to a patch of weeds about ten feet away. "I saw it happen. There's no way to make that pretty."

Danny opened the passenger door. He didn't know what

to say to that and figured there probably wasn't anything he *could*. "You need to get to sleep. We got work in the morning."

He shut the door after JD tumbled inside, and as he made his way to the driver's seat, he couldn't quite believe how right Pablo had been earlier at Lincoln Park.

You can make art happen anywhere.

Danny looked over at JD. His cropped hair made him look both younger and older somehow. He was already snoring.

CHAPTER TEN

DANNY CAN'T BELIEVE THAT ROXANNE CAN'T BELIEVE IT

"I can't believe this was even your idea," Roxanne said, wiping beads of sweat from her forehead. "And I honestly thought you'd be shit at it."

"Shit at pulling weeds?" Danny drove a hoe into a patch of yellow brush, the blade disappearing into the tangle. He pulled on the handle, breaking a thick stalk loose and revealing a bald patch of dirt. "Who can't pull weeds?"

"I was guessing you," Roxanne said. "I never pictured you as the manual labor type."

"Bro, I landscaped my entire backyard. I mean, the Sarge brought in all the rock and plants and stuff. Had this big ol' plan for what it was gonna look like, but then he made me do everything. Said a backyard should be a place to get away from work . . . except for me, I guess."

"Is Tío finally gonna relax for once?"

Danny tossed the thorny mess—about as big as JD's little

brother—inside a half-full trash bag and surveyed the area. They were clearing the yard faster than he'd thought they would, it almost halfway done already. Danny checked his watch, wondered if JD was going to show like he'd said. He'd texted him a few times already but gotten nothing back. "He took the next week off, if you can believe that."

"I do believe it. No way Tía was gonna let him go back to work. I mean, why waste his last week—" Roxanne cut herself off. She looked fast at JD, her face pinching with apology. "I don't mean like his *last* week."

"I know what you mean," Danny assured her. Heart surgery. His father needed *heart* surgery.

"Have you told Tío about the mural?" Roxanne twisted the heavy-duty trash bag she was holding, making a perfect knot at the top. It was fat in the middle with garbage.

"Not yet," Danny said, appreciating her changing the subject. "I don't want to stress him out with my bullshit right now."

"You shouldn't call your work bullshit," Roxanne said, annoyance in her voice. "I mean, you're fixing something, right? You're making something *actually* better." He'd told her about the change of plans that morning, her liking the idea right away—even if she still wasn't cool with him using the credit card.

"The Sarge cares about me making good grades," Danny said, knowing that wasn't exactly true. "That way, in some distant future, I can make good money. He's been on that since forever."

"Yeah, my mom kinda thinks the same way," Roxanne said.

"Wants me to use my *potential.* She's still super mad I'm going to Community. I mean, she doesn't say that out loud. But she constantly has disappointed-mom-face."

"That's the Sarge's whole vibe—his *why did I work so hard for you to only do this face,*" Danny said, stuffing his trash bag with more dead plants. He paused, then asked, "Do you feel guilty about not leaving for school?" all while checking his phone. Nothing from JD. Last night Danny walked him to the front steps of his nana's, where he puked all over his own shoes. JD didn't have a key to the house, so Danny had to ring the doorbell and wait for JD's mom to unlock the door, looking both half-asleep and fully pissed off as she helped carry him inside.

Roxanne must have noticed Danny checking for messages because instead of answering his questions, she reminded him, "You said that's JD's car up front. He'll have to show up sometime to get it."

Danny nodded, shoving his phone back in his pocket. "Yeah. You're right."

"And I don't feel guilty," Roxanne continued musingly, jumping back on Danny's question. "I really wanted to go to Middlebury. I think being in Vermont would be cool. So would going to UCLA."

"So why didn't you? You never really said." Danny paused, thinking. "But I'm glad you stayed, if that means anything." He again thumped the hoe into the ground, listening for the satisfying crack of the weed's stem, then pulling it up by the root. He wondered if his prima was now his best friend; he hung out with her more than anyone else. She came today just because he asked, the way Juan and JD would have, once upon a time. JD was probably super hungover, but he wasn't answering texts and last night he didn't seem to want to help, not really.

Roxanne tugged out some dried-up-looking dead plant, a sunflower maybe? "It's hard to explain," she said. "I know everyone thinks it's only because of Juan. And me staying *has* a little to do with Juan dying, how he died. Why he died. I think about what happened. I think about him. But that's not the whole reason I'm still here."

Danny held the bag open for her. "Did you . . . ? Did you start getting scared like all the time?" he asked. "Like almost right after?" Danny remembered the months after the shooting. Fear had seeped inside his bones, like the hard desert ground absorbing an overdue rain. Seeing cop cars cruising by fucked with him every time. They *had* to be following him. He was sure that at any second they would flash their lights, and anything could happen after that. Danny quit driving the very day he noticed a cop behind him on the way home from school. The squad car tailing him for miles, turn after turn, Danny squeezing the steering wheel so hard at ten and two his hands ached afterward, and his sweat soaked into the upholstery of his seat. Staining it.

"How could anyone not be afraid after what happened?" Roxanne said gently. "But that's not it either." A pained expression crept across her face, like she had something to say but it was stuck in her throat.

Má had to start driving Danny back and forth to school, and the only reason he ever got behind the wheel again was because of the Sarge. *Just because you've decided that you don't drive anymore doesn't mean you don't work on your car.* The Sarge forced Danny to get in the garage and change the oil and rotate the tires. Flush the transmission and brake fluids. And after every task was complete, they rode together, the Sarge making Danny drive, telling him to listen to the engine and the shifting gears as they circled the neighborhood. *Do you know what courage is?* the Sarge had asked during one of their trips around the block. *It's doing what's hard. Always be brave enough for the hard road.*

Danny shook his head, remembering this. His father was so confusing. He elbowed Roxanne. "Yo, homes, I'm still waiting for you to *actually* say something. And I promise that's not me trying to talk shit. I want to know."

Roxanne paused, a new weed in hand. "What does it matter?"

"Because everyone else is gone." Danny almost choked it out. "Except for us."

Roxanne tossed the weed in the trash bag and flung it beside another stuffed bag. "First off, *I* got friends. And second, you can't help but talk shit. It's, like, your only skill." She leaned over and grabbed her water bottle from the ground. It was covered with stickers. EAT THE RICH. PEOPLE OVER PROFITS. ABOLISH ICE. She took a long drink, then looked back at Danny. "Fine. To answer your question. I stayed because of what Juan was doing when he died. He was risking everything to go on a road trip to meet his dad for the first time."

"The dude wasn't even his father, though!" Danny said too fast, with too much edge in his voice. "I mean, that part was really fucked up."

Roxanne popped open another trash bag, began thrusting

her arms into the thorny nests and yanking them out one by one. "Everything else about that night was. What he was trying to do *wasn't*. Like, the trip was more than meeting just one person." She stayed crouched in the thicket of thorny goatheads, her arms now lined with scratches, cuts. "Think about it. Juan had the Senior Day game coming up. He was gonna get the scholarship he'd always wanted. But he needed to know who his father was first."

"But he was never gonna know," Danny said.

Roxanne took another drink from her water bottle before handing it to Danny. "That's not the point. He didn't *know* that."

Danny grabbed her bottle, gulped some water down, his throat dry. Lips cracked. They had been working since dawn, starting in the cold dark and steadily going as the desert heated up. They were using the empty dumpster at the end of the alleyway, chucking fat trash bags, the spiky leavings, the empty booze bottles inside. Just part of the mess Juan's dying had left behind.

"He wanted *family*. He chose to go see his dad over all that other stuff," Roxanne said. The brightness of her face clouded over. "If I had never met Juan, I might've gone away to college without really knowing how important my family was to me. *That's* why I stayed. For a little more home. At least for one more semester."

Danny plopped down beside his cousin, passed her back her water. "What do you mean, one more semester?" The fall semester was coming to an end, and he had barely made it through—he may still not make it. "Where are you going?"

Roxanne's face brightened again, her grinning. "I'm going back to school in the spring, taking my scholarship at UCLA."

Danny was stunned.

He didn't want her to leave.

To be gone like Juan and JD. "I thought you liked working with your mom and dad."

"That doesn't mean I was gonna become a baker." Roxanne balanced her water bottle on the palm of her hand like a scale. "We don't automatically become whatever our parents are."

Danny lightly slapped at Roxanne's hand, knocking her bottle to the ground. "Are you sure about that?"

Roxanne glared at her cousin, grabbing her water and wiping it off. "I do feel happy in the bakery. It's true. I love the smell, the powdery feeling of flour on my fingers. But what I really love is talking to the customers. I like listening to them talk about their lives, about birthdays and weddings coming up. Jobs and kids. They tell me—for some reason—every detail on how they're feeling and how it's impossible to find a doctor close to home. So, I've decided I'm gonna be one. Open a little clinic right in the neighborhood."

Danny felt tears pooling in his eyes, and he couldn't tell if he was sad or glad. He had to turn away, looked out at the yard and the building in front of him. Until now the place had turned into a field of overgrown spike bushes and broken glass, a building of empty rooms with busted walls. The decay had come so quickly after Juan died, the place seeming to die right along with him.

"Well, that's good news," he said at last. And it was, even if the idea of Roxanne leaving felt terrible. "You'll be a badass doctor."

"Yeah, no shit," Roxanne said, standing, stretching her back. "I guess JD ain't coming. I mean, we're making a dent in this, but some help would've been good."

"Doesn't look like it," Danny said, hopping to his feet as well. "He was a complete mess yesterday. Something's up with him."

"More than usual?" Roxanne side-eyed Danny. "Seriously, that dude is like a sad song come to life."

"But like an emo one," Danny said. "One that's more embarrassing than sad."

Roxanne laughed, then flexed her hands, which were probably feeling as tight as Danny's did, and surveyed the yard. "Still, I don't know if we're gonna finish today without the mope's help."

She was right. Danny still needed to clear the last quarter of the dead vegetation and trash. The walkway needed clearing, too, a path to observe the mural at just the right distance. He looked to the busted back wall. He could set some of the pieces of the busted concrete into the path. He saw the path leading through the yard—to the mural. This was where his work—all of it—belonged, on buildings instead of hidden inside them.

"Let's do as much as we can," Danny said decidedly. "While we have the time."

CHAPTER ELEVEN

BOOKS AND BADASSES

JD hosed the puke into the rocks, washed off the rest of Nana's porch while he was at it. His memory from the night before was fuzzy, only bits and pieces coming to him. Amá said Danny had brought him home, woke the entire house banging on the front door. She'd nudged him off the living room couch at eight in the morning and handed him a cup of coffee, telling him to clean his mess outside. Amá's anger was just below the surface, where she always seemed to keep it, her words becoming sharp and pointy.

JD's head was pounding. Holy shit.

Pops had been at the house the night before. JD remembered he'd been inside, with Amá, then back on the porch talking his bullshit. About his wedding the following weekend and how life had moved too fast for him. That must have crushed Amá. She thought Pops still loved her, maybe even wanted him to.

"Do you wanna go to church with me?" Amá was asking now. She joined JD outside, looking ready in her usual Sunday outfit, a black button-down shirt and black slacks, hair pulled back in a bun. He killed the water. At least the puke smell was gone.

"Not this time." JD coiled the hose neatly by the spigot and reached for his coffee, took a sip. Not now, not ever again. Not that he was going to tell Amá that. JD hadn't stepped foot inside a church since Juan's funeral, and it was hard for him to not still feel angry at almost everyone crammed inside the church that day. Fuckin' fakers. He and Juan had roamed the halls of Austin High together for years, almost no one ever paying attention to them, but suddenly a roomful of basically strangers were all tears over Juan dying, as if they really knew anything about him. Like that he liked hanging with his grandpa. Or secretly wanted to be a comedian. Was afraid of swimming pools but wanted to one day see the ocean. Actually *liked* clowns. That all he wanted was a family.

The scene had reminded JD of his First Holy Communion. Back then Amá had told him that after taking the Host he would know God for the first time, would actually *feel* God. JD had been excited that morning, even though Amá had slicked his hair to the side and dressed him in a suit like a little businessman. But as he took the Host, dry and sticking to his tongue, he felt something very different. *Nothing.* As he walked back to his pew, he watched the kids in his row. No looks of joy or excitement, no one freaking out about meeting God. The whole thing was pretend, everyone faking because they were supposed to.

Amá sat on the porch swing, the metal hinges groaning as

she glided slightly back and forth, watching him put away the hose. "Are you going to be here when I get back?" JD remembered promising Danny that he would help pull weeds—*why on earth would he do that?* He thought about the girl he'd met, Isa. Wondered if he should text her. And he really had to get back to DM. He had work the next morning. Ten days, he thought. *No, eight now.*

JD joined Amá on the swing, causing it to rock abruptly and her to grip the armrest and cluck at him, but she didn't complain much more than that. JD knew he was a total pain in her ass. And that she was—while not super patient or all that forgiving either—*there* for him, just like Danny had been the night before. She maybe, in some way, she *was* his home. "No, Amá," he finally answered. "I have stuff to do before I go back."

"You always got stuff," Amá huffed. "Everyone's got their *stuff*."

"I'm guessing Pops told you about all his bull-stuff, then?"

Amá reached over and squeezed her son's hand. Gave him a thankful smile. "He told me you embarrassed him at dinner. That all he was trying to do was be nice and take you out for your birthday. And that I need to stop turning all you kids against him."

JD slung his arm around his mother and pulled her close. Gave her a squeeze. "I got him pretty good."

Amá leaned in, seeming to enjoy the moment, then stood up. Posture straight. Her expression hard and focused. She was ready to go. "Remember, he's your father. You should show him respect."

Respect. It amazed JD what a one-way road *that* was. "Okay, Amá. I'll try."

Amá's face softened as she looked down at JD. "I'm sorry I called you a fool." She looked at her watch and dug into her purse, pulled out her car keys, her running late for Mass. "And for saying that—"

"I'm deploying," JD cut her off. "I leave in eight days."

Amá jolted, squeezing the keys, her beater Chevy Aveo's alarm—parked in front of Nana's—chirping. She stumbled backward, appeared disoriented, then regained her composure. Shit. JD should've told her earlier, not with her running out the door.

"Where are you going?" she asked, composing herself, patting at her bun, tucking it tighter.

"Have you been watching the news?"

"Oh no, mijo." Amá seemed suddenly unsteady again, taking another step back, then another. JD rushed toward his mom, wrapped his arms around her.

"I'll be fine, Amá. Like I told you the other day, I'm just like you."

The backyard looked amazing, which kind of freaked JD out. He could see Danny and Roxanne, raking piles of pulled thorny debris and garbage, stuffing them into plastic bags. He'd thought about sneaking over to his car, slipping inside, and quietly driving away unnoticed. But that would be shitty. Danny had been texting all morning, asking when he was going to come. Then if. JD never responded, deciding instead to pack his overnight bag, say goodbye to Nana and Tomás, and then walk over.

"Looking good," JD called out as he approached from the alley. There was a tightness in his belly that squeezed the closer he came. With the weeds and trash gone, the yard looked almost like it always had. He could picture himself in it, Juan and Danny. He could picture that night.

"About time," Roxanne called out. She ran up and hugged him. It was good to see her. "We didn't think you were coming."

Danny was glaring at him. JD guessed he should've messaged back, but the thing was, the idea of messing with Juan's old place just felt *wrong*. It still did. But seeing it—like it had been—wasn't as bad as he'd thought. "Thanks for taking me home last night."

"You got puke all over my shoes," Danny complained. He was leaning on a rake, only a few feet away from where Juan had fallen to the ground. Neat rows now lined the dirt, no sign of what happened. The blood and bullet casings were long gone, but at least the confusion of overgrown spikes and thorns and out-of-control trash were a chaotic clue that *something* had gone wrong here. A kind of scar that was now being removed.

"My bad," JD apologized. "And sorry for not answering your texts. I was still pretty unconscious. I zombie-walked over here."

Danny nodded at JD's bag. "You leaving already?"

"Yeah. I gotta get back. It's a five-hour drive."

"That's not too long," Danny said.

"You should come back next weekend," Roxanne suggested. "Your boy over here is gonna be painting a mural."

Danny tossed the rake, a plume of dust rising as it slapped

against the ground. The neat lines disturbed. "He doesn't think I should do it."

JD's head *and* stomach ached. He wanted to sit down. To get in his car and blast the AC. To drive the fuck away. "I don't remember saying that, not exactly." His memory was still fuzzy, but he thought he'd said he wanted to leave it the way it was, wondered why things had to change.

"It'll be kind of like a memorial," Roxanne added. "That way no one will forget about Juan."

"I don't know about a memorial exactly," Danny explained. "I'm not sure exactly what it'll be."

"Do what you want," JD said with a shrug. The dark red brick of the building had always stood out in the neighborhood. The bricks seemed fancy, like they should've been used to build a castle somewhere else and not a crap apartment building in Central. "I was drunk as fuck and talking shit last night. Why were you even listening to me?" JD flashed Danny the palms of his hands, scratched and cut from shards of glass the night before. "I mean, what happened here?"

"Bro, I got nothing to say about that." Danny laughed. "But you should come next weekend. Isn't your dad getting married, too?"

"Oh, you gotta come for that!" Roxanne exclaimed.

"I'd be cutting it close," JD said. JD had no idea what the next week at work would be like, if he would even have any more time off. "I deploy next Monday."

"What?" Danny gasped, the color draining from his face. He seemed to go paralyzed, standing stiff as the rake he'd been holding. "I don't even know what to say to that. Fuck."

Roxanne's face went stormy. "This shit never stops. Like, some kind of war has been going on for our entire lives. How fucking brutal. Like for what even?"

JD had no idea. Not about the reason. Not about how brutal any of it was going to be.

JD was on the road when he got the text.

Isa: **What the bundt are you doing right now? You should meet me at the bookstore, we can get a stupid cake afterward, if you're cool.**

He was surprised to hear from her so soon and decided what the hell; it was just a quick detour. He found her curled up in a comfy-looking chair in the fiction section, her focus on the page she was reading. It was exactly where they'd been the night before and the first place JD had thought to look for her.

"Well, look who's a smitten kitten," Isa said without taking her eyes off her book.

"Meow?" JD immediately regretted playing along.

"You are so weird!" Isa exclaimed correctly. She slipped a bookmark into her paperback and shut the cover. JD studied her expression, wanting to figure out if she thought he was the good or bad kind of weird. She had a sly smile going, a mix of amused and flirtatious. The truth was, JD *was* a smitten kitten. Sure, Isa was fine as hell, with long impossibly black hair and perfect teeth, her bottom row crooked in the cutest way. Her nose was thin and her cheeks sharp, her eyes a honey brown. But it was her bold and sure-of-herself way that had JD right where she wanted him—at least he was hoping that she wanted him.

"You don't speak cat?" JD said. "Speaking multiple languages is a sign of badassness."

"I took a year of it in high school," Isa deadpanned. "But my teacher was a dog. I think he was the football coach, and they just made him do it. He also seemed kinda racist."

"Was he always telling you how cats were lazy?"

Isa shifted in her seat. She was reading *Dominicana* by Angie Cruz. JD didn't read, not that he was against it. He quickly scanned the stacks and stacks of books, realizing that if he wanted to start, he would have no idea where to begin. "It was more subtle. Like he once told us he only bit Mexicans."

"That does seem racist," JD said, looking at the empty space on the shelf where the book he'd gotten had been, frantically trying to remember the title. "I bought that book."

Isa gracefully stood up and motioned for JD to follow, leading him down the fiction aisle. "I checked."

"I haven't started it yet. But I will." JD hadn't even thought about reading it until the words popped out of his mouth. He would take it with him on the deployment. Give himself something to do—even though he had no idea what kind of free time he'd have.

"I've never read it," Isa admitted. "I just grabbed one off the shelf."

"Maybe I'll buy the same one you're reading too."

Isa stopped and playfully slapped JD on the shoulder. "Are you asking me to join a book club with you? We haven't even had sex yet."

"Oh shit." JD clapped his hand over his mouth, eyes darting around and waiting to be shushed like he was in a library.

Talking with Isa was like being on a roller coaster, exhilarating in the best possible way. "How about I just buy it and read it, and maybe, if we're both into it, we can talk about it?"

"How about you buy me a coffee?"

They sat at the little café inside the store. Isa, drinking her chai latte, explained how she worked at La Malinche part time and went to school at Community in the nursing program. The plan was to start off as an LVN and then go for RN down the road. That sounded cool to JD, who poured sugar into his bitter-ass coffee until it was breakfast-cereal sweet. He told her about being in the air force, how he was leaving soon. She seemed bummed, which, oddly, made JD feel a little better about leaving.

Isa walked JD back through the bookstore, wanting one more go-around before leaving. She ran her finger along the spines of books as they made their way through the stacks. "I get the sense you don't really read, so you need a good base." She grabbed the Angie Cruz and one by Louise Erdrich, *The Sentence*, handed both to JD.

They continued.

She snagged *Sing, Unburied, Sing* by Jesmyn Ward, *How to Live Safely in a Science Fictional Universe* by Charles Yu, and *The People of Paper* by Salvador Plascencia. "These last two are a trip. Read them last."

"Okay," JD agreed. He would've agreed to anything.

After a cashier rang him up, a plastic bag of new books in his hand, he walked Isa to her car. They stood by her driver's-side door. It was their first awkward moment, neither of them seeming sure what to do or say.

Isa broke the silence first. "Will I be able to call or text or whatever?"

"Yeah, I'm pretty sure," JD said. "I might come back next weekend." He didn't know why he said that.

"That would be cool," Isa said, giving a shy smile. JD leaned in slowly for a kiss, and Isa gave him her cheek. She took a step back at him, her expression part apologetic but also defensive.

JD also took a step back, nodded. He understood. The way they'd been talking, fast and funny, was part defense. A little bit of armor because silence was so damn hard. And saying what he wanted was even harder. "I'd really like to see you again."

"Slow down, Book Club." Isa winked at him, opened her door, and got halfway in. "But, seriously, that sounds nice."

"Drive safe!" JD called out as he watched at Isa fasten her seat belt and crank the engine on her old rust-bucket, it coming to life after a few turns of the key.

"*You* better hit the road," Isa said, pulling away. "You're gonna run out of daylight."

The house was empty, which was probably for the best. The spare key was in the nicho, just like always. Amá's hiding places never changing, no matter where she lived. JD really should've been on the road already, but after seeing the cover of *Dominicana,* he knew Amá needed the story inside—JD totally judging the book by its cover. There was something about the woman on it, her face troubled in a way JD recognized. A look Amá sometimes had.

JD placed the book on her bed, scribbled a note for her:

Amá,

I bought a bunch of books for the deployment, if you can believe that. I got this one for you. Don't get mad if it sucks. And please don't be mad at me anymore.

Juan Diego.

42

LA CALAVERA

"Al pasar por el panteón, me encontré un calaverón"

"Get inside. He's awake."

Apá called out to Daniel from inside the house. He was in the backyard with Fernando, them watching the chickens run around and kicking a flat soccer ball back and forth. The whole family was at Tata and Nana's, the little red brick house just a block away from the Sunset Grocery in Sunset Heights. His older cousins had gone to shoot hoops at the busted asphalt court that overlooked the freeway, leaving him and Fernando behind. His primos were all in high school, some already finished. Either graduated or just *done*. Daniel and Fernando were the youngest of all the primos, meaning no one really wanted them around. Daniel squinted into the window where he'd heard Apá's voice coming from, the rusty brown screen making it hard to see. "Why are you making that dumb face? ¡Apúrate!"

Tata was dying.

That's what Amá told him and Fernando before the drive that morning. That Tata had been sick and for the last two days couldn't get out of bed, a nurse now coming to the house to watch him. It was Saturday, and Daniel had wanted to go riding his bike to the park and see if Angie might come by with her brothers. Angie hung around on the swings while her brothers beat their brains in playing tackle football. Her brothers were cool, but Daniel was more interested in Angie. She was in seventh grade, just like him, but went to Basset Middle even though she lived in the neighborhood. She told him all about it once while gliding back and forth on the swing. Going higher and higher. She told Daniel that she was in band and played the French horn. How she was in gifted-and-talented, which meant her homework was harder but that was actually a good thing. Daniel liked to hear her talk, but what he liked even more was not talking. No need to explain how he had become radioactive at school. So much so that even his once best friends Hector and Miguel now pretended they didn't know him. How he had two fake teeth.

But no bike ride today, no Angie. The entire family was crammed inside Nana and Tata's room. Tío Rudolpho and Tía Gloria. Tío Dago and Tía Ana. Tía Helena and Tío Manuel. Everyone either sat or stood by the two small beds in the room, one Nana's and the other Tata's. Amá sat on Nana's bed, and Apá stood at the head of Tata's, him perfectly straight and still, like he was a bodyguard. Tata's eyes were finally open, but they looked weird. Like a pair of light bulbs dimming and about to flicker out. Daniel couldn't tell if Tata was really awake; his breathing was short, halting. The room seemed to be holding its breath, like everyone was saving the air for Tata. The nurse wiped Tata's forehead with a wet washcloth—her breathing normal as could be.

"Say something to your Tata," Apá said as the two boys settled in beside him, Apá looking intensely at them. "Let him know that you're here."

"I'm here," Daniel said obediently.

"Not like that," Apá snapped. "Say something good."

Beside Tata's bed on the wall was a picture of Apá from his army days. He looked much younger, the same age as Daniel's primos were now, but in his uniform he somehow looked like a man. Tata must've been proud, him keeping Apá's photo so close to his bed all these years, his other sons and daughters relegated to small picture frames propped on his dresser.

Daniel knew Apá wanted him and Fernando to show respect, to look at Tata because he was dying and prove they were being raised right. Outside the chickens were scratching around in the dirt, making their clucking noises. The low sound of cars zooming along the freeway hummed in the distance. Daniel wanted badly, so badly, to be outside. To run toward the basketball court with his primos, not to play but instead watch the cars speed by. To pick a random car and imagine the anywhere else it could be going.

But soon the sounds of chickens and highway gave way to sobbing. Tata's eyes were still open, but they'd suddenly frozen, becoming dull. Fernando started crying. Just like Nana and now Amá. Everyone in the room wept, except for Apá and the nurse, who was busy folding a towel and placing it under Tata's chin to keep his head from rolling on its side. Apá looked at Daniel and nodded approvingly. Daniel, like his father, with a face as hard as a rock.

CHAPTER TWELVE

DANNY GETS TO WORK

The hatchback was crammed with all the gear Danny needed as he drove down the highway. Drop cloths and old towels. Painter's masking tape, rollers, and paint trays. Brushes and pallets. Chalk. His cans of paint, acrylics in all sorts of bright colors, and of course a white latex base. The scaffolding he'd rented was set up and ready to go at the back of the building. He'd cleaned up the rest of the yard and laid out a winding walkway, leading from the alley to the back patio. Sunday evening he'd used the busted rock and chunks of concrete from the collapsed wall, setting the former rubble into the ground like a mosaic, leaving the back of the property open, welcoming.

A few of the neighbors started to take notice. They'd come out into their own backyards to take a peek before returning inside, satisfied he wasn't there to make something bad even worse. Last night, the man who lived next door had even come over. Danny told the old dude about the mural. How the back of the building was going to look like a Lotería tabla, with three cards on the top floor, three on the bottom, and one in the center. Everything about the señor was thin. His arms and legs. His short white hair and the skin around his neck and elbows. He'd told Danny *it was about time someone did something* and handed him a bottle of water. Said he was a good chamaco, like his son.

Danny hoped the neighbor was right. That he was, in fact, doing *something* and not what he was afraid he was actually doing. *Screwing everything up.* It was already Tuesday, the week before finals, and Danny had zero plans to attend classes. Danny emailed his Econ professor. Then his TA in biology. Asked what *exactly* did he need to get on his exams to squeak out a C? And then there was Pablo. He wondered if this was what the dude had in mind for his three paintings—not that it freaking mattered. The Sarge's surgery was on Friday, and school seemed so unimportant.

Danny exited the highway on Piedras and was making his way through Central. The streets were mostly empty, a few cars putting along on the narrow road. Probably on their way to work. Stopped at a red light, Danny swiped through some photos he'd taken on his phone. Looking at the different murals around town he'd snapped pictures of. The blue woman near the convention center. The Rock House Gallery wall in downtown. The sisters, two young women so close they could be Siamese twins—Juárez and El Paso—cloaked in cactus-green gowns. Roads into each city at the hem of their dresses. That image was painted over brown brick on Father Rahm Avenue, and it was his favorite.

Yesterday he'd rolled out a layer of white base paint and then outlined the top floor, La Muerte, El Borracho, and La Dama, and sketched out the bottom row, El Pescado, El Soldado, and El Venado. El Corazón right in the middle as the sun had been going down. Today he would start to paint.

The image of El Corazón had come to him while he'd been hammering plywood over the broken windows. He'd been replaying Dr. Rivera's words in his head: *I think we should also go for an elective aortic valve repair. . . . I just think it's finally time.* Time, he thought.

In the original Lotería image, the heart was muscular, veiny. An arrow piercing through it with a single drop of blood on its tip. Danny had placed his hand over his own heart after driving the last nail into the plywood, listened and felt for the beat. All the shattered windows were now covered, the wood painted to match the red brick on the outside of the building. As he stood with his hand on his chest, he started to think of the heart as a clock, a timepiece. With perfect gears and fittings that, when aligned, accounted for every moment in a life. Each beat counting upward toward an unknowable future.

But what happened when one of those gears broke, a tooth cracking and snapping off? The clock would stop, time breaking still. Everything suddenly going all wrong.

Danny parked in the back of the apartment and popped the hatch. He loaded his milk crates full of supplies into his old Radio Flyer wagon (that Má had kept all these years, jeez) and pulled it all into the yard. The wagon rattled along the mosaic path. Danny had already measured out precisely where he would paint the Lotería cards, the white rectangles now equally spaced out on the back of the building, the base layer dried, and the images already sketched in colored chalk.

La Muerte was first. Danny climbed on the scaffolding and poured bright yellow paint into an empty plastic butter tub and mixed it with some red and orange until it became the earthy yellow for the skeleton. In another he created the dark blue of the police uniform by adding a deep purple to his steely blue. He breathed in the smell of the paint, the chemical smell soothing, calming, as he painted in La Muerte's face, being extra careful to apply the color evenly on the brick. Was this how Roxanne felt while inside the bakery with Tío Fernando? "Happy" was the word she'd used, but to Danny, doing the work felt different. "Satisfied," he thought, maybe was the word.

"No way I would've guessed it was you," a voice from below called out.

Danny looked down and, no way. No way. Standing in the backyard was his art professor. Pablo, in a hoodie and jeans, him *still* wearing those scuzzy Chucks. What the fuck was he doing here?

"Are you like stalking me or something?" was all Danny could think to say.

Pablo had his arms folded across his chest, hands tucked into his armpits, nodding his head as he gazed at the wall. "My apá told me there was a young kid next door who reminded him of me. Said you were working hard on a painting or something. Wanted me to come check it out."

"I guess your dad doesn't like critiquing as much as you

do." Danny studied Pablo's expression, his face serious, eyes focused on the artwork in front of him.

"That's a recent development," Pablo said, nodding in agreement. "You're also not his son."

They stared at each other, sharing a *you get it* look. "Your apá told me he was glad I was doing this, which is probably the nicest thing anyone has said about my art. And I haven't really started yet." Danny dipped his brush in the tub for more paint.

"I'm glad you're doing it too," Pablo agreed. He walked closer, then farther back, taking it all in. "You seem to actually care about this, which is all I was trying to get you to do in class. That, and not being such an ass."

Danny lightly flicked his brush at Pablo's feet, spotting his teacher's old shoes with drops of yellow paint. "Well, you failed that part."

Pablo didn't flinch as the droplets cut across his feet. "Dude, I'm an artist *and* a teacher. You can't possibly think I've given up working on you. Look, if you finish this project, you pass. Let's see what you got."

Danny felt that feeling again—satisfied—as he began to paint. There was something about creating outside on his own, instead of in Pablo's classroom or school. Here his work wasn't cliché or being done just for a grade. It was part of his life. But he would be letting everyone down if he just quit college. What if he decided to take a break instead? Roxanne took a semester off. Why couldn't he? Danny could already hear the Sarge's voice in his head: *Do you know what courage is? It's doing what's hard. Always be brave enough for the hard road*. But both roads, staying in school, quitting to paint on his own, seemed impossibly hard. "That hallway assignment is still whack," Danny said, turning to Pablo.

"How are you getting that yellow?" Pablo asked.

"I just mixed in some red and orange with my base," Danny said. "I wanted Death's body to look like bad teeth."

Pablo nodded. "That sounds perfect for Death."

"What kind of student were *you* at school?" Danny asked, turning around and getting back to painting, suddenly nervous to look Pablo in the face. "I bet you were good."

"Remember when I told you that all you had to do was care?"

"Yeah," Danny said with a laugh. "Who forgets crazy advice like that?"

"School is where I learned that, to care about my craft." Pablo walked around Danny's equipment, trying to check out the paint colors. "You're just learning that in a different place."

Danny set down the yellow paint and grabbed another tub, started on La Muerte's body. Him filling in the oily blue uniform. The paint shone vividly on the wall. "But everyone *cares* if you finish college, don't they? I'm supposed to be the first one in my family to graduate. My mom and dad have worked their whole lives for this, and I'm fucking that all up."

"I got a son," Pablo said, seemingly out of the blue. "I showed you a drawing of him in my office."

"Your cubicle," Danny interrupted.

"Right." Pablo laughed. "But that's actually my point. I teach at the college. But I also do freelance ad work. And then I work on my own art. I do all that for my son."

"You sound just like the Sarge—my dad." Danny focused

on Muerte's arm, wanting to capture the bony joints underneath the uniform. "But he likes that shit. He's always liked being at work."

"That's because he's Mexican," Pablo said with a shrug. "That's what we do. Me. My apá. You. That's what you're doing right now. Work is a gift we give to the people we care about."

Danny clenched his paintbrush. "I don't think I want to go to school anymore."

Pablo folded his arms across his chest. Took a breath. "Look, college is supposed to make life better, safer. Your education is supposed to keep you safe from joblessness. From working outside or with your hands for long, brutal hours. For brutal people. My apá thought that. I *still* think that. Sending you to school is maybe the only way your dad knows to show you that he loves you." Pablo glanced behind him, and sure enough, his dad was in his backyard, leaning against a workbench and smoking a cigarette. What looked like an old turntable was scattered across the bench in pieces, it next to a set of small screwdrivers and a multimeter.

"Are you gonna do that to your son?" Danny asked. "Even though you know nowhere is actually safe?"

"I know your friend died here," Pablo said plainly. He looked to Danny, who was also watching as his father began tinkering with the turntable.

"Was murdered," Danny corrected. "Juan could've had a college degree. The cop wouldn't have cared. He would have shot Juan no matter what."

"That's true." Pablo's face looked resigned. "I'm sorry

about your friend. But maybe the reason you're on that scaffolding right now, the reason you're doing all this work, is because you also can't think of a better way to show how much you loved your friend. So yeah, I'm probably going to do the same for my son. I'm going to teach him. And love him. And *work* for him. What the fuck else are dudes like us going to do?"

45

EL VENADO

"El venado, no ve nada"

"They didn't even see me do it," you complain.

"But you did do it?"

"Yes."

They sit you at the Sarge's favorite booth at Good Coffee, which ironically has terrible coffee. You have no idea why your father loves the joint. The eggs are too greasy, the refried beans soupy. The bacon is almost always burnt. Nothing in the diner is actually *good.*

The Sarge studies the menu as if he is going to order anything other than his usual huevos rancheros with the runny beans and a cup of awful coffee.

"If you call your restaurant Good Coffee, shouldn't the coffee actually be good?" you ask, wanting to be funny and change the subject.

"It's aspirational," the Sarge says. "Like 'Live, Laugh, Love' or 'Rest in Peace.'"

"Since when are you funny?"

"I retire in a month," the Sarge says. He takes a sip from his coffee, winces as the brew passes his lips. He is in uniform, has again picked you up from the principal's office. "I need a hobby."

"I only sprayed a little." You try to explain, but you know that won't fly. You did it on a dare, pressing the trigger of the pepper spray in the main hallway. Mr. Pokluda, the assistant principal, was trampled as students rushed to get outside for air. JD laughing as he choked.

"They're gonna expel you, you know?" Your father doesn't even look upset, which is suddenly way scary.

"You should yell at me. Why did you even bring me to breakfast?"

The Sarge smiles, and you can tell by the way he does it that he isn't as mad as you thought. You pick the menu, not really hungry for anything. "Everything looks so good," you say with way too much enthusiasm.

"Get the huevos rancheros," the Sarge says. "They're almost never cold."

"Is this what being an adult feels like?" you ask, putting the menu down. "Playing a different kind of make-believe?"

"Mostly," the Sarge says. "It's a combo of that and always being tired."

"¿Listos?" the waiter says.

He brings a basket of chips and salsa, tops off the cups. The man doesn't smile or ask how anyone's day is going. He doesn't have a little green notepad or pen to take down orders. Your father rattles off his usual, plus a small bowl of menudo.

You order the same and watch the waiter turn and slowly walk off, ignoring a couple in another booth wanting his attention. "They should call this place *Good Service*."

"The service has always been bad," the Sarge agrees. "But the food . . . it's barely okay."

"Why even come here?"

"Because your tata used to bring me here on Sunday mornings, after selling furniture at the swap."

You wonder about Tata, him dying before you were born. He is a collection of framed photos. Of half stories. More of secret than a myth or legend.

"You don't talk about Tata all that much."

"My old man wasn't as easygoing as I am," the Sarge says with a snort. "He worked all the time, but we ate here together. It's my favorite memory of him."

"What did you talk about?"

The Sarge scoops a chip heaping with salsa into his mouth. "We didn't, not really. You know, I always thought I'd be a different kind of father than he was."

"I don't know anything about him."

"You know more than you think."

The waiter returns to the table, sliding hot plates of huevos rancheros in front of Danny and the Sarge. He also hands them napkins and silverware. He pauses for a second, raising his eyebrows as if to say, *¿Algo más?* When no one says a word, he leaves.

The Sarge is right about the huevos rancheros. They're actually pretty good. You spoon some salsa verde on top of the eggs and take another bite. "I thought I was going to be in big trouble."

"You are."

You watch your father eat. In a month he'll be out of uniform. No longer the Sarge. No more deployments. Just Dad.

"So am I, like, grounded or whatever?" you ask.

"Nothing like that," your father says. "I'm enrolling you in Catholic school."

He takes a sip from his coffee.

You take a sip from yours. "Maybe you could send me to prison instead."

The Sarge digs into his breakfast. "No. I like the school uniforms better." He forks at his eggs, the yolk runny and red with salsa. "And you'll actually spend less time praying than you would in prison. So, you're welcome."

7

LA ESCALERA

"Súbeme paso a pasito, no quieras pegar brinquitos"

1. The process starts with a rosary. There you will meet family members who remember you as a baby but that you don't remember at all. They will talk about Tata like he was either a saint or the devil. They will do it right in front of you.

2. At the rosary, a dude who is not your priest will lead the praying. Only the women know the words, and even then it's only the old ones. Amá will look both angry and embarrassed praying alone. Apá will sit stoned faced the entire time. Copy him exactly as Fernando squirms in his seat.

3. In the middle of everything, the not-priest will stop to lecture everyone for not knowing what to say. For being too sad for church. He'll tell everyone they need more church, and Apá suddenly looks like he did in his army photo. Ready for battle.

4. When it's finally over, take your turn to look at the body lying in the casket. Pretend it is somehow still your Tata. Say goodbye to the empty shell now wearing his favorite guayabera. Look as sad as everyone else but don't cry. Don't cry for decades, not until the day your wife leaves you, taking your son with her.

5. Later that evening sneak into the backyard where, Apá and all your tíos are downing beers. They won't notice you grab a can and take your first drinks. They'll only laugh and laugh as you stagger around later that night, the stars you love so much spinning above you like they're in a blender.

6. In the morning put on your best clothes—even though you know your cousins from California will make fun of them. When you get to church, everyone will be serious—last night still pounding in their heads. A real priest will talk about Tata, but everyone will be able to tell he doesn't know a thing about your grandfather. That, like always, the priest just wants to talk about God.

7. At the cemetery no one will know exactly what to do with themselves. Most will just hide behind sunglasses and avoid looking at the coffin and the hole in the ground. The ones with real small kids will drift after them as they run off to play. After the funeral, everyone will go searching for headstones, looking for graves, for loved ones they haven't thought about in years.

8. Back at Nana and Tata's, everyone eats. Go to the backyard and see the chickens. Tata loved them. Wonder what happens to the birds now that he is dead. Wonder what happens to all the things a person loved once they are gone forever.

9. Listen to everyone having a good time. Listen to them say that it shouldn't take death for family to get together.

10. Repeat these steps when Nana dies a year later.

CHAPTER THIRTEEN
JUST ONE MORE BOMB

"Take it down. Do it again." Hermosillo stood in front of the jet. He'd finished going over the bomb, making sure Rowe, Raines, and JD hadn't missed a step. They'd been loading the same munition since the morning, only now they weren't in the semi-controlled environment of the Load Barn. They were on the flight line, with running aircraft around them. Power units—massive generators almost as noisy as jet engines—rumbled as maintenance crews hooked them up to broken airplanes and performed diagnostic checks. A thick layer of gray clouds stretched across the sky, hanging just above the mountains and blocking the sun.

"Whatever you say, boss," Rowe huffed. He had convinced the chief to send him to the war, but not before Hermosillo had one more chance to put him—and his crew—through his paces. That's the way things seemed to work in the military. If one person had a tantrum, everyone got spanked.

So they loaded again.

And again.

And again.

Lightning streaked across the sky, the bright flash cutting across the darkening clouds. Thunder followed. JD loved Arizona storms. The smell of rain on the concrete and desert ground. The sound of furious drops pelting the earth. A pair of vultures sat across the flight line, perched on top of a hangar and seeming to watch the crew work. By now all three of them appeared to have figured out what they were doing. Even Rowe now able to follow a checklist, while Raines and JD could now move bombs back and forth from the trailer and load them onto the stations in their sleep.

But being good with one type of bomb wasn't enough. A green tug pulling a trailer, stocked with missiles, pulled up. A driver hopped out, a young airman—her no older than JD—disconnected the trailer and drove off. Then another tug showed, left an ammo loader full of bullets for them. Hermosillo waved as that tug driver pulled away.

"This is bullshit," Raines said. The flight line was clearing out, maintainers were heading inside. They'd been at it all day. Loading bomb after bomb. The work had seemed endless. Brutal.

Hermosillo walked over to Raines and JD. "What do you think it's gonna be like over there?"

Rowe stood by the missile trailers, looking the projectiles over.

"I've been. *Twice*," Raines said, annoyance in his voice.

"Yeah, me too, but the kid hasn't. And neither has he." Hermosillo nodded over to Rowe. "What does *that* tell you?"

"Man, that's not my fault."

"Sure isn't," Hermosillo agreed. "But it's our problem. Shit like this always is."

The clouds opened up as the first missile slid onto the wingtip. The three of them had lifted it off the trailer and walked it to the jet, careful to avoid gashing themselves on the sharp fins, moving cautiously so they wouldn't drop it. They had four more to do. The rain was cold, thudding down and rolling off the slick skin of the aircraft. JD took a quick glance around the flight line. They were the only ones left. The vultures gone too. Even the vultures had gone?

"We're not done!" Hermosillo yelled over the storm, as if reading JD's mind.

They got the last three up, and then JD and Rowe pushed the ammo loader toward the jet. It was heavy, thirty-millimeter rounds weighing it down. JD watched as Raines attached the contraption to the aircraft and began transferring the bullets from the loader into the plane. *Is this what it's going to be like?* He was drenched. Exhausted. He'd been worried about getting good at his job, but he never thought about what that meant. About bombs dropping and missiles firing. Bullets shooting. People dying. Dead, and because of him.

"Sanchez!" Rowe struggled to push the loader by himself but couldn't. "C'mon, man."

JD helped shove the heavy machine away from the airplane. The four men stood silently, looking at the fully loaded jet. With missiles and bombs, it looked menacing, like an animal baring its teeth. The rain poured, thunder cracking as lightning flashed overhead. The vultures were back, circling above, round and round.

CHAPTER FOURTEEN
CAUGHT IN A BREEZE

It was time.

Friday.

Surgery day.

The waiting room was packed, groups of nervous adults quietly poking at their phones, everyone silently agreeing to ignore a collection of kids climbing over chairs and running back and forth. The walls of the room had been painted pink, the color choice probably meant to make the space seem pleasant but instead made it seem like they were stuck inside a bottle of diarrhea medicine.

Danny sat wedged between Má and Roxanne, his tía Carmen off getting coffee. Tío Fernando yawned, his mouth opening wide, but he quickly covered it with the palm of his hand, probably not wanting to seem inconsiderate, or worse, bored. Altogether they'd been at the hospital for seven hours now, the Sarge in surgery for almost six. Danny guessed that pretending you didn't have such normal feelings when a loved one was being cut into by strangers was the least they could do. Still, Danny knew exactly how his tío felt.

He'd been buzzing with nervous energy earlier in the day but was now bone tired. He was, in fact, struggling to keep his eyes open. Even though he knew his father's life was on the line, his eyelids kept fluttering. He'd been getting up before dawn all week, going over to the apartment and working on the mural. He was almost done. The La Muerte was finished. Danny's version of Death now boldly overlooking the neighborhood, the reaper in his cop uniform and mirrored sunglasses that reflected the curvy scythe he held in his sickly, bony hands. The skeletal fingers tightly curled around the wooden handle. Danny'd painted La Muerte's background a pinkish melon, just like the original Lotería card, mixing a bright red with white. With a plop of yellow. Stirring and stirring until he had the color just right.

El Borracho was complete too. As Danny'd been sketching the image on the wall, he realized the face he was drawing was JD's. That this painting had become a portrait of his friend slouched by the broken window in Juan's old room, a 40 in his hand. Danny had brightened JD's eyes as he painted, highlighting the moonlight that had reflected in them through the busted window that night—what, a week ago?—subtly adding flares of white against the brown textured irises. He also lightened some of the shadowing he'd made in his original sketch, softening JD's face. He was hurt, Danny knew. Not just angry. He knew, because JD was also—him.

Pablo had come over again, wanting to help. So Danny

let him fill in the backgrounds on El Venado and El Pescado. He had to admit how dope the ripples in the water looked against the twisting body of the fish, a hook yanking against its mouth. La Dama ended up looking just like Fabi, her face with the same vacant look she'd had when she'd given Danny her Lotería cards. El Soldado only needing some final touches. To add the explosions over the mountain ranges in the distance. To darken the night sky. Danny had finished the most important part of the painting. His tata's young face. He'd sketched the portrait from memory, darkening some of the shadows of his face to make him look both hard and scared while dressed in his service uniform.

Danny wanted his mural to be seen from far out in the neighborhood. For it to call out to people like the highway ones did and make Juan's old place more than an abandoned building or crime scene. To make it—okay, fine—art. He'd flared his brushes as he painted, leaving behind confident strokes and textures on the wall. He felt like a baker sprinkling flecks of sugar on a fresh-baked empanada.

Pretty much all Danny needed to do now was finish El Corazón. The gears inside the heart needed to be perfect. To look complicated and precise. Delicate and durable. Danny had already painted the background. A warm yellow he got by mixing it with some red. The heart outlined directly in the center. He'd also stenciled the number 27, and EL CORAZÓN in their proper places on the Lotería card. Last night he'd again sketched out the gears, then resketched them. Then one more time. He'd been out there into the evening, almost missing dinner with the Sarge and Má, which was longer than he wanted.

• • •

"I bet she's lost," Roxanne whispered to Danny.

"Who?" Danny said, shaking his head out of the daze he'd been in.

"My mom," Roxanne said. "I'm pretty sure she needs Google Maps just to make it from the living room to her bedroom every night."

"She's in a hospital," Danny said. "What bad thing could possibly happen here?"

"All sorts of bad shit." Roxanne scoffed. "Like, people die here all the time."

"Hopefully not today," Danny said, raising an eyebrow at his cousin.

A horrified look spread across Roxanne's face. "I swear I didn't mean anything by that!"

Of course he knew she didn't mean anything by it. That she was trying to distract him. To make him laugh. "I'm just fucking with you," Danny said. "That was a decent joke . . . for you."

Roxanne reached her arm around his shoulder and pulled him tight. He was glad she was there. That he wasn't going through this all alone. A giant TV mounted on the wall was muted, but the screen had been cascading with new images of explosions and footage of soldiers walking onto the back of a cargo plane. Each one loaded up with gear. A reporter, standing at the foot of a mountain range, was talking into her microphone and looking over her shoulder, as if she expected something to suddenly explode.

"Let's go find your mom," Danny said, looking away from

the screen. "I need to move around. We've been sitting for way too long."

"That's a good idea," Má said, suddenly coming to life in her seat and apparently listening to everything Danny and Roxanne had been saying. She slapped Danny on the knee before standing. "Carmenita surely needs a rescue party by now." But it was Má who looked like she needed rescuing. She looked newly shipwrecked, her face tired yet panicked. Like she wasn't even sure where she was.

"I'll wait here." Tío Fernando yawned. "In case Carmen miraculously finds her way back."

Together the three of them walked down the now familiar but still confusing hallways of William Beaumont, and it didn't take long for them to get turned around. The military hospital had a different vibe than other hospitals. Danny couldn't really describe the difference, and he wondered if that was because he was a civilian. He'd been around the military his entire life, an army brat for sure. But he didn't know what being *in* was truly like. The Sarge had made that clear the other night when he told him to promise to never join. That he didn't want him to ever find out.

"I swear that cafeteria is just around the corner," Roxanne insisted. "That's where she went, I'm sure."

"This place is like an Escher painting," Danny said. "But even more boring."

"We should go back," Má suggested. "What if the doctor comes to the waiting room and we're not there? The surgery has been going on for too long."

Danny decided to scout ahead and check one last hallway,

turning and going down another identical corridor, quickly leaving Roxanne and Má behind. Then he stopped in his tracks. Má had been right to be worried, because coming toward him was Dr. Rivera, striding at a determined clip. Still wearing her surgery scrubs, her plain square framed glasses, she seemed to be the exact kind of person the Sarge could trust with his heart. Everything about her all business. Her face betraying nothing.

"Hey," Danny called out, about to ask how his father was.

"Mr. Villanueva," she said first. "I can't find your mother. She's not in the waiting room."

"She's right behind me," Danny said. But when he jogged back around the corner, Má and Roxanne were gone. He hoped they were making their way back to the waiting room.

"Come with me to the ICU," the doctor said. "I can let you see him for a minute and update you on the surgery."

"We gotta find Má first," Danny said. "Let me at least text her."

"I'll send a nurse to find her." Dr. Rivera was already walking back the way she came. "We should get going."

The Sarge was out of surgery and still unconscious. Dr. Rivera said he'd be out for another four to six hours and would need constant monitoring. That she just wanted him and his mother to see that he'd made it through so they could relax a bit. Standing between the hospital bed and the bank of monitors and machines wired to his father, Danny tried to focus on what Dr. Rivera was saying, but it was hard to pay attention. The Sarge's face was surprisingly swollen around the eyes and nose, his lips pale and dry. The scar under his eye still fresh. There were little wires and drainage tubes poking out of his chest, a breathing tube down his throat.

Danny wanted to cry.

Dr. Rivera explained how the surgery had gone. That she'd made a nine-inch incision across the sternum and then carefully replaced the damaged portion of the Sarge's aorta with a graft, a tube made of Dacron, which she carefully sewed in its place. Like the Sarge, she talked with her hands, as though replaying the surgery in her head and not wanting to miss a detail. Danny could tell how important this—his dad—was to her. It became obvious to Danny that she was a soldier too. A Mexican one. That her work was what she offered to the world.

When she determined that he was following along, Dr. Rivera continued. "After we replaced your father's failing valve with the porcine bioprosthesis, we had to install a temporary pacemaker. There was some atrial fibrillation, which is not too unusual, but it's something we're going to monitor because of the risk it poses."

"Okay," Danny said, not knowing what else to say. What she was saying sounded scary, but Danny had no idea if it was or if it was just him being afraid. Or if it was just technical mumbo jumbo. Danny glanced out into the ICU hoping to see Má walking in. She would know, would be able to ask Dr. Rivera the right questions. The unit was shaped like a horseshoe, the patients' rooms—open, with only privacy curtains to shield them from onlookers—lined the outside. Nurses' stations were cubicled in the center, complete with banks of computers and cluttered workstations. The Sarge's curtain was drawn back, leaving him exposed. "Can I go get my mom now?"

Before Dr. Rivera could answer, the different monitors connected to the Sarge—that had all been beeping in a calm, steady rhythm—started to become erratic, sounding off one after the other like car alarms during a storm. Nurses suddenly appeared, rushing toward the Sarge from their stations. Dr. Rivera turned from Danny to analyze the blinking numbers and jumping lines on the displays of the monitors. Nurses zipped around, scribbling notes in their charts and marking times on a dry erase board mounted to the wall beside them. Earlier, on the bottom right corner of the board, someone had drawn a happy face and written *smile* in big purple letters. The machines kept blaring, the sound like electronic cymbals crashing.

Smile. Danny couldn't think of a crueler word. Of anything more hurtful or wrong. Smile.

"Clear the room," Dr. Rivera ordered tersely as she reached for a pair of latex gloves. She looked over at Danny, her face softening before turning to a nurse. "Please get the son out of here. And find his mother." Underneath the white sheet, Danny noticed his father moving, his unconscious body curling his arms and legs toward his chest. A nurse gently guided Danny by the shoulders and walked him from the room, pulling the curtain closed behind them.

"Go on back to the waiting room," she said, pointing toward the exit. "We'll come and get you as soon as we're able." She disappeared behind the Sarge's curtain just as Má walked into the ICU. She ran toward Danny. The worry Danny, the Sarge, and Má felt the night before was now here, the barrier no longer invisible. Danny studied the thin curtain separating them from his father, the commotion on the other side causing it to flutter like it was caught in a breeze.

36

EL CAZO

"El caso que te hago es poco"

"Do you know that boy?" Apá asked. "You keep looking at him." Daniel sat next to his father in the army recruiter's office, the two of them shooting the breeze about future careers.

Infantry. Military police. Helicopter repairer.

"No," Daniel lied. "Never seen him before."

It had been forever since Daniel had seen Adán Flores, the dude getting expelled for biting Ms. Mora, the eighth-grade English teacher, and never being heard from again. As he'd started his freshman year of high school, Daniel had been worried Adán would eventually show up, along with the story of Daniel getting the teeth punched out of his head, but neither ever did. It seemed the only person who still remembered the fight was Daniel, him now a senior who thought about that afternoon more than he wanted to.

Adán sat next to a junked-out Toyota Tercel parked a few spaces from Apá's truck—an old but clean F-150 that Daniel had worked on with Apá since forever. Him learning to change the oil and brakes.

Replacing a fuel pump and rewiring the ignition switch. Adán's car looked to be in bad shape, with dings and dents along its body, its white paint along the back bumper stained nearly black, coated by burning exhaust. Adán looked hopeless, sitting on the ground, the car's hood popped open in front of him like an open mouth ready to gobble him up.

"That boy's father failed," Apá said, now watching Adán too.

"He doesn't have a dad," Daniel said.

"I thought you didn't know him," Apá said, raising an eyebrow.

"I mean, probably," Daniel added quickly. "It doesn't look like he was being forced to help tune up an old truck before learning how to ride a bike."

"I guess if he had a bike, instead of a car, he'd be on his way," Apá said matter-of-factly.

"I get a bunch of recruits like that," the recruiter added. "Or ones with a stepdad. Kids really hate stepparents."

"Hmm." Apá grunted. "Sounds to me like they should bring the draft back. Get some better recruits."

Apá had been drafted, Daniel knew, but he didn't really know much else about his dad's army time. He'd done a tour in Vietnam that he never talked about and after that lived in Germany for a few months. But Apá talked so little about the army that the only evidence he'd even been in it was the one photo of him in uniform, now stashed inside his closet after Nana died. On the way to the recruiter's, Apá would only say that being in the army would be good for him. That he probably should've stayed in himself.

"I'd be out of a job if the draft came back, Mr. Villanueva," the recruiter said, chuckling to himself before turning serious. "I like doing this job. Helping those young people out . . . You know, if we go with Infantry, Mr. Villanueva, we can have Daniel ready to go right after graduation."

Outside Adán had hopped to his feet and jumped in the driver's seat of the Tercel, tried starting the engine before getting back out and looking inside the engine bay, then smacking the side of the car hard and again taking his seat back on the ground, his head slumped.

"What about a job without the guns?" Apá answered for Daniel. "Why don't you teach him something that he can use in the civilian world? You know, for after the army."

"Well, Mr. Villanueva, Daniel's test scores just barely meet the minimum for helicopter repairer," the recruiter said apologetically. He smiled at Daniel, the same thin and unsure smile Jessica Portillo had given a month earlier when she'd said yes to going to the prom with him—but only as a friend. "I don't want him to make it all through Basic just to end up failing at AIT."

"The kid can turn a wrench," Apá said, switching his attention away from Daniel and the recruiter and back outside, toward Adán and his stalled car. "Some people are good at tests, and some at getting things done."

"We both want Daniel to get a job he'd like," the recruiter agreed.

It didn't seem to Daniel that either man cared that what *he* wanted was a job studying the stars. But Daniel's SATs were no good, his best grades in school only Bs, even in science. Maybe helicopters were as close as he would ever get to them.

"Go outside and get that car started," Apá suddenly said to Daniel. He was making the same face he made on Saturday mornings at the swap. The *this is the price* look he gave cheapskates who wanted to haggle over a one-of-a-kind piece of furniture.

"What?" Daniel said, knowing there would be no negotiating. "Why?"

"Go outside and get that car started," Apá said again. "Go finish what you started."

How the hell did Apá know? Daniel smoothed his tongue over his front teeth, flung himself up out of the chair, out of the office, and tentatively walked over to Adán and the broke-ass car. Daniel knew he wasn't the same kid Adán would remember from seventh grade. Puberty had worked on Daniel like some kind of comic book accident—like his now six-foot-tall body had been blasted by gamma rays or bitten by a radioactive spider. Daniel used his new powers to play tight end on the football team. And while not especially good at catching the football, he did have a talent for blocking. For clearing a path for a running back by slamming his new body into defenders and knocking them off their feet.

Adán slowly stood as Daniel approached. The inside of his car was in just as bad shape as the outside, the dashboard with a long crack running across—just like the windshield—and stuffing showing through the fabric of the sun-bleached back seats, groceries from the Bag 'N Save across the parking lot piled on them. Once the baddest dude in seventh grade, Adán already looked past his prime. As if by high school he'd already turned Apá's age. His once broad shoulders were slumped, his hard muscles gone soft. Even his face seemed old, tired. Still, he puffed his chest out as Daniel approached. Of course Apá and the recruiter were watching from inside the office; Daniel could feel their eyes on him. Could see Adán's trying to look right through him.

The boys eyeballed each other, neither of them saying a word. Adán obviously recognized Daniel now, his shoulders thrust back as he tried to make himself big. But Daniel loomed over him. He'd been getting ready for the army all year—that was the only reason he played football. He'd been lifting and running. Spent hours punching on the heavy bag Apá had hung in the garage. He needed to become a warrior, Apá had said. Not just to make it in the army but just to make it.

"Try starting it again," Daniel said, not taking his eyes off Adán.

"It doesn't start," Adán said, all smartass. "Why do you think I'm sitting here?"

"Because you don't know shit about cars," Daniel said.

"What did you say?" Adán snorted, taking a step toward Daniel. He looked like he had that day in PE when he'd tripped over a basketball and belly flopped on the asphalt, everyone on the court laughing at him, his face like an angry bull's right before charging.

"I said you don't know shit." Daniel also took a step, him now in Adán's face. "So, you can grab your keys and try it again, or you can sit here and let all that food you got go to shit." He remembered how he'd once run away from Adán. How everyone ran away after their fight, even Adán, but they weren't those same kids anymore.

Just as surprising, Adán got behind the wheel. The car made a clicking sound as he turned the key. Danny peered down at the engine. The bay of the Tercel was an oily mess, almost every part coated with black grime. "Turn on the lights," Daniel said. The headlights flashed on, a dull yellow glowing from behind the hazy lens. Daniel walked over to the driver's side and peeked inside, Adán moving back in his seat. Giving him room. The dashboard lights were flashing, the CHECK ENGINE light a bright steady yellow. "You got any tools?"

Adán popped the trunk and hopped out of the car, was back seconds later to hand Daniel a black plastic case he grabbed from inside, the thin handle cracked, one of its plastic locks missing. Daniel opened the socket set. More than half the tools were missing, only a ratchet, a few sockets, some open-end wrenches, and a screwdriver remaining. The battery terminals were corroded, so Daniel got to work, first on disconnecting the cables and wiping the bluish-white gunk away with a rag that had been jammed inside the socket set.

"Your battery is leaking," Daniel said at last. "You're gonna want to clean the terminals with baking soda and water. But what you *need* is a new battery." Apá spoke like this whenever they worked on the truck, him always matter-of-fact and never really explaining, Daniel and Fernando always trying to figure out what the hell he was talking about. Next, Daniel inspected the battery cables and was surprised to see they weren't brittle and ready to snap. The insulation still good. He reattached them to the battery.

"So, you can't get it started either?" Adán said, him now looking into the engine bay as well.

Daniel had almost forgotten Adán was even there. That Apá and the recruiter were watching from the office window. As Daniel checked the connection at the starter—making sure it was secure—it surprised him how much he wanted to fix the junker. To hear the engine turn over and roar back to life.

"You see the starter?" Daniel pointed it out with the screwdriver. "I'm gonna crank the engine. If it just clicks, you're gonna give it a good tap with this handle and I'll try again." Adán nodded as Daniel handed him the screwdriver, then jumped inside the driver's seat. As he turned the key, the car made the clicking sound, only this time faster, like a faint pulse starting to come back. "Okay," Daniel said, turning the ignition back off. "Give it a tap."

"Okay," Adán said, lightly tapping on the starter.

"Try it like you're not afraid," Daniel said, climbing out of the driver's seat and quickly crowding his old bully by the engine bay. He stood inches away from Adán, looking at him, then at the starter. "I remember you hitting harder than that."

"I don't get what you mean," Adán said, trying to move away from Daniel and the open hood.

Daniel grabbed Adán by the shoulder and shook his attention back to him. He balled a fist and pounded it against the palm of his other hand. "Like this hard," Daniel said. "Do it three or four times."

Adán stood motionless, his face twisted in confusion, as if he'd suddenly found himself losing a fight, seventh grade having happened in the early rounds and now these going to Daniel. Daniel had taken his hits and survived, had never stopped moving forward and was now firing away. Adán looked down, took the screwdriver, and thumped the starter.

Whack. Whack. Whack.

Back in the driver's seat, Daniel turned the key and listened as the engine struggled, then coughed to life. Apá stood outside the recruiter's office, shaking his head in delighted disbelief as a grin spread across his face. He and Daniel listened to the engine—it knocking, struggling to keep running. Daniel thought of the night Apá taught him how to throw a punch and realized all the things hands could do. Remembered what Apá had said just right before.

You're a Villanueva.

CHAPTER FIFTEEN
DANIEL VILLANUEVA

A nurse had scrawled the Sarge's name across the plexiglass of the isolation room, an inconspicuously enclosed patient room tucked away in the corner of the ICU. Caution stickers lined the only entrance, warning of infectious and immune diseases. Masks required. The Sarge was sequestered inside, intubated and on a ventilator. Drainage tubes still sprang from his chest, slowly dripping away fluid that was collecting inside him. His body was broken, fragile, like an injured bird's nested in the middle of a tangle of cords all wired to him and jumping monitors. Danny watched him from the other side of the plexiglass, from an adjoining office where doctors and nurses constantly monitored the patients inside.

Má was in the isolation room with the Sarge, folded into a chair that Dr. Rivera had wheeled inside for her. Má looked to be asleep. The room was small and cold, the humming of machines, the occasional beeping and mechanical breathing of a ventilator, made a weird music, but far better than the nightmare orchestra that played twenty-four hours ago, twenty-four hours ago when his father had a stroke and Dr. Rivera and a team of nurses went into crisis mode. Frantically saving his life—at least for now.

Dr. Rivera had requested the Sarge be put in the ISO room so her team could better monitor him. She told Má and Danny that hyperfusion of his brain must have occurred during the surgery. The arterial fibrillation he'd experienced also a likely probable cause. She wasn't sure. But now the Sarge was unconscious. His brain swollen inside his skull.

"The edema could get worse in the next few days," Dr. Rivera had said carefully. "We're treating it, but the worry is that he'll need a hemicraniectomy, and at this point he may not be strong enough for the surgery. We'll have to make that call quickly if or when the time comes."

"Can he hear us?" Má asked, seeming to ignore every word Dr. Rivera had said. "I want him to know that we're here. That he's not alone."

"I like to believe that he can," Dr. Rivera said, trying to sound reassuring. "So, talk to him. Hold his hand. Keep him tethered to the world he knows and loves. That's as good anything we can do at the moment."

It was quiet in the little office beside the ISO room, minus the offbeat plunking of a leaky faucet. The skeleton night shift crew made their rounds, nurses peeking inside recovery rooms and checking on sleeping patients, monitoring vitals. Danny and Má were the only overnight visitors. The glow from

Danny's tablet lit up the small office. He was working on a new card, number 37. El Mundo. Danny had searched online for the original image—a man holding the world across his back, the weight of it taking him down to one knee. Danny didn't sketch the man like he was in the original, young and muscular, the world seemingly not *too* heavy. Instead, he drew his father, his face wrinkled as he grimaced, struggling as he carried everything. His hair, the stubble on his face, a mix of black and white. His body not up to the job anymore.

The morning of the surgery, the Sarge had surprised Danny by coming into his room. He was already dressed for the operation, wearing his loose-fitting Dallas Cowboys T-shirt and a pair of sweatpants. His glasses and baseball cap. Danny was still in bed. The sun wasn't up, outside pitch-black. No way it was even close to time to go. But the Sarge was always—*always*—early.

"What's up, Dad?"

The Sarge reached out his hand, taking ahold of Danny's. His father's hands were rough—dry and cracked. His fingers were bent, the joints swollen, arthritic from years of turning wrenches. They trembled inside Danny's. "I just wanted to talk, before everyone was awake."

"Okay," Danny said, sitting up, his muscles tensing, nervous energy taking over. His father's hands were still shaking, the movement slight. Did they shake like this all the time and he hadn't noticed? Danny wondered. "What's up?"

The Sarge's eyes became watery; he quickly pulled his hand away from Danny and wiped the tears from his eyes. "Do you remember the day your mom said she was leaving?"

Danny nodded. Of course he remembered. Má moved them to El Paso and in with Nana two weeks later. It was weird being in a place that Má called home but to him felt strange and foreign. Meeting people she'd said were family but he'd never met. She tried telling Danny how much everyone loved and even missed him, but he understood it was her they loved and missed. He was more of a lost dog she'd come home with.

Má was a different person in El Paso. Her and Nana always talking in Spanish, making each other laugh. Danny never having any idea what they were saying. Danny began to feel as if he were invisible, until he met Juan and JD. Luckily, his dad joined them a year later, still in the army but able to transfer to Fort Bliss. Able to try to fix things.

"That was the worst day of my life," Sarge continued. "I'd let your mom down. I let you down. I had started to think that my only job was to make a future for you both. And not, like, an everyday life."

"You do talk about school and work all the time." Danny pulled himself out of bed, sitting next to his dad. "But that's okay. We fix cars too. Do stuff."

"Yeah, all sorts of stuff." The Sarge smiled sheepishly at Danny. "I remember the day you were born. I held you in my arms in a recovery room, and it felt like I was carrying the whole world in my arms. Except the weight of it wasn't heavy. You were light and delicate and absolutely perfect. I promised that I'd protect you, that I'd give you everything I never got as a boy"—he wiped at his eyes again—"and instead all I did was weigh you down with the exact same nothing."

The Sarge patted him on the leg and stood to leave. Danny could tell his father was trying to say goodbye in case things didn't go right, but he didn't want him to. He wanted him to stop talking. Everything is going to be just fine.

The Sarge stood at the door. "Whatever you decide to do with your life, know that I'm already proud of you. That I love you."

Danny looked at his drawing one more time and then put it to sleep. He thought of the shades of blues and greens he could use for earth's oceans. Cobalt and azure. Cerulean and turquoise. The white and grays for the clouds swirling over the masses of land. He packed up his stuff and joined Má and his father in the isolation room. Má didn't move, her soundly asleep as he stood beside the Sarge and gently picked up that rough, calloused hand and held it.

"I love you, Dad," Danny said. "Now just come back. Come back, like you always do."

35

LA ESTRELLA

"La guía de los marineros"

Daniel was back.

Fernando picked him up at the airport. He looked too young to be driving the old F-150, his sixteen-year-old face still with a trace of baby fat, but he maneuvered through the jam of cars along the pickup and dropoff lane like he'd been driving for forty years. One hand on the wheel, whistling softly to himself. Once free from traffic, he told Daniel about how he'd found Apá in the garage, working on a set of kitchen cabinets. Their father had made it over to the stool he'd kept in the corner before the tissue in his heart started dying on him, his arteries suddenly blocked by clots. *He was probably trying to sit down,* Fernando explained, *catch his breath, but instead collapsed to the ground. The stool knocked over beside him.* Fernando hadn't known what to do, seeing Apá laid out like that. Not moving. Not saying anything as he called Apá's name and then, instinctively, for his big brother, Daniel.

But you were gone, you know?

It was a Friday, the day before the funeral. The army had let Daniel fly home for the weekend, the rosario already happening while Daniel was in the air. Amá was mad Daniel wasn't there, or so Fernando said. That he was just like his father. Work always mattering most to Villanueva men. The army had told Daniel his training would continue the following week. They warned him if he didn't get back on Sunday, he'd get washed back or maybe kicked out altogether.

Fernando was still dressed nice from the rosary, tucked in and sporting a tie. His hair combed and neatly parted. Daniel wondered who'd done his tie. Whether Apá had taught Fernando, like he'd done for Daniel shortly before Daniel left for boot camp. Said if he was going to make it in the army, he needed to care about everything, from cleaning and assembling a rifle to perfectly tying a tie.

Fernando was softly singing along as Apá's old tunes played inside the truck, the music barely audible above the engine rumble. Like all Mexicans, Apá enjoyed the shit out of a sad song. Fernando and Daniel rode in silence, both of them lost to remembering as Los Lobos played:

No sé cómo decirte; no sé cómo explicarte; que aquí no hay remedio, de lo que siento yo, de lo que siento yo; la luna me dice una cosa, las estrellas me dicen otra, y la luz del día me canta esta triste canción.

Esta triste canción.

Once at the house, Daniel and Fernando gravitated to the kitchen. Them drinking Apá's leftover Tecates, squeezing limes and salting the tops of the cans. After a few beers, Fernando decided to make empanadas, for after the funeral. *I remember how Amá made these for Tata's funeral,* Fernando said. *How everyone said they were his favorite. I ate them with Apá, just me and him. He said they were his favorite too.*

Daniel watched as Fernando worked. He had a recipe—a sheet of paper written in Amá's handwriting, it pulled from an old envelope with others neatly folded inside—but his brother didn't seem to need it as he fired up the oven and started measuring flour. He then carefully added brown sugar and cinnamon to the pineapple he now had simmering on the stove. Fernando looked as natural in the kitchen as Apá had in the garage.

He must've just lit a cigarette right before, Fernando said as he started to knead the dough. *It was still burning on the ashtray when I found him. And then—I don't know why—but I picked it up.* Fernando described how he held it between his fingers the way he'd always seen Apá do. That he let it burn until the long ash dropped from the butt.

The two brothers went silent again. One baking, the other drinking. Both feeling how loss gripped the body. Daniel seemed to ache from head to toe, but the feeling was worse in his chest. A tightness just starting to grow.

With everything quiet, Daniel could hear weeping coming from Amá's room, as soft as a sad song. She'd gone to bed shortly after giving Daniel the hardest hug of his life outside on the porch, and as she'd squeezed, her face buried in his chest, Daniel looked up at the night sky with its clear bright stars scattered across it like sprinkled sugar. As Amá walked back inside the house and disappeared into her room, Daniel remembered how Apá would sometimes look up at the stars in amazement. Daniel had always thought his father really didn't understand what he was looking at. The stars weren't really there after all, each light its own little lie.

But it was Daniel who had gotten it wrong. He could see now that starlight was actually a reminder. That even if it came from a star that was long gone—its heart exploding out in the universe—every night brought its memory, a bright and brilliant chance to remember it had existed at all.

5

EL PARAGUAS

"Para el sol y para el agua"

FOR GOOD TIMES AND BAD: A CHECKLIST

☐ **Pay Your Dues**

Look for Apá. Remember that everyone buried in Fort Bliss National Cemetery was a warrior. The etchings on the tombstones mark World War I and II. Korea and Vietnam. Desert Storm. Feel relieved when you find your father. When his tombstone tells you what he couldn't: *Jose Luis Villanueva, SPC, US Army, Vietnam, Purple Heart.*

☐ **Save**

Save your money. Save your leave. Send as much as you can to Amá and dump the rest into an account you don't touch. Listen to Sergeant Troncoso, the old dude who tells you to start a Roth IRA. Who says: *Don't be like all these other stupid motherfuckers that don't get shit from being in the army. Have a fucking plan.*

☐ Be All You Can Be

Work those Black Hawks. Pull engines and rotors. Slap in gear boxes and transmissions. Flight controls. The boss tells you the helicopter is named after some Indian dude. Look him up. Ma-ka-tai-me-she-kia-kiak. Discover he was not the son of a chief or medicine man but instead made his own way as a warrior. His a melancholic and unwavering life fought for the tribe. Make this your plan.

☐ Leave

Drive home from Kansas for a long two weeks off. Stop at truck stops and two-pump gas stations along the way. Eat shitty food and spend a night in a rat hole motel in Tucumcari. Learn more about America, mile by mile, than you ever could in school.

☐ Meet a Girl

While on leave, ask Fernando what's up with his lady's friend. *Is she with anybody or what?* Let him laugh at you from behind the counter of Carol's Bakery, where he now works. He says: *Just talk to her, bro.* Talk to her and instantly forget how mad you are that Amá bought Fernando a stand mixer and other baking tools with the money you send for the mortgage. How Fernando is an artist just like Apá.

☐ Get the Girl

Remember these two weeks for the rest of your life. Fernando and Carmen, Sandra and *you.* Remember how hard you fell in just fourteen days. Spend your time apart trying to remember each moment. Your time together trying to relive them. Be fine with a long-distance thing, be fine with a lot of things.

☐ Get Insurance

Sign up for the life insurance and wonder how these companies even make money. Everybody dies, after all. Then freak out that you're suddenly worth more dead than alive. That this fact will be true until the day you actually die.

☐ **Go to War**

Don't listen when the old guys tell you to dump your girl before leaving. Tell them Sandra ain't like that and listen to them laugh. Don't worry about the war, they say. They've seen this all before. The buildup. The waiting. The enemy rolling over faster than your girl.

☐ **Pretend**

Ask Sandra to marry you right after you come back from deployment. Pretend you don't notice how unsure she looks when she quietly says *Yes.* Pretend you're not suddenly more nervous than you were before asking. Before deploying. Before joining the goddamn army.

☐ **Don't Get Mad**

Don't get mad when Sandra hates Kansas and then Virginia even more. Don't get mad when after Amá dies and leaves you both the house—and you give your half to Fernando—he sells it to buy the run-down bakery he works at. Don't get mad when Sandra leaves to El Paso and takes your son and the future you've been working for. Don't be mad that no one can see the plan but you.

CHAPTER SIXTEEN

SNITCHES GET . . . WHATEVER THEY WANT

"So what you're saying is the motherfucker can *finally* read a checklist?" Curtain slapped JD on the back and chugged his can of beer.

"He checked all the little boxes and everything?" Peterson gave JD a playful shove. "I don't believe it."

They were in Hermosillo's backyard, a farewell party in full swing. It turned out Hermosillo was way more Mexican than JD had given him credit for. He was hooking up a carne asada, grill billowing smoke as he flipped the thin steaks, Ramón Ayala cranking on a portable speaker, and the dude was singing along like an uncle at a quinceañera.

JD sipped his bottle of water. "I mean, we loaded enough times. *Fuck.* We were there all day."

"That shit was hilarious." Curtain killed his beer, tossed the empty into a giant rubber trash can, the can rattling against the others collecting inside. "You and Raines should get Purple Hearts for that."

"All the colors." Peterson tossed his empty too. "Go get me another one."

Hermosillo lived away from base, on the west side of town in a little house near the mountain. Juan's mom, Fabi, actually lived close by. She'd moved to Arizona after Juan died, becoming a student at the same community college where Juan had been planning to go. She always cooked Juan's favorites whenever JD'd come over, and they would spend their time talking about him. JD liked hanging out with her at first . . . but had stopped visiting over time, the meals starting as pleasant trips down memory lane but eventually becoming dead ends. Fabi's and JD's lives going in two separate directions.

Like Fabi's, Hermosillo's backyard faced out into the desert, a thicket of mesquite trees and palo verdes. Creosote. There were saguaros too. They lined the side of the mountain, their long green trunks lined with spikes, arms stretching upward, heads crowned with flowers. JD had been running a nearby trail all week, past rows of the giants—some over ten feet tall—that gave him a feeling of excitement and joy each and every time.

Curtain clapped his hands together. "Who wants another one?"

JD raised his water bottle in the air and shook his head. "No, thanks."

"It's your last Saturday night before a deployment, and all you're gonna drink is water?" Peterson eyeballed JD curiously. "You're the weirdest dude. I'll take two, then."

Curtain cut across the yard, and JD spied Rowe standing at the opposite corner with his wife and son, a teen shrouded in a hoodie and lost in the blue light of his phone, earbuds probably blocking the sound of his dad, who was talking loudly at him. Kid was probably only a year younger than JD, if that.

"I doubt that," JD told Peterson. "But the last thing I'm gonna do is give homie over there a reason to fuck with me."

"Glad he ain't in charge of my crew," Peterson said. "He's a total clown, bro."

"But is he, though?" Raines chimed in, joining them, bouncing a tiny baby in his arms, the bundle wrapped in a pink blanket, little matching knit hat pulled onto her head. His new baby girl. "He wanted to deploy, and now he is, even though he completely sucks at his job." Raines looked directly at JD. "He's gonna get the special-duty pay. Free leave when he gets back. And the whole time we're over there, we'll be the ones doing all the actual work, his crew—the Black guy and the Mexican kid?"

JD watched as Raines continued bouncing his baby up and down, pacifier in her mouth, little hands balled into tight fists. He was a brand-new father. Starting a brand-new life and this deployment coming at the absolute worst time. "I'm fucking sorry, man."

Curtain strolled up, arms cradling cans of beers. He handed one to Peterson. "What I miss?"

Peterson cracked it open. "Oh, nothing. Just Raines making everything racial and JD being weird. Normal shit."

Come to think of it, so much was happening, or would be, while JD was deployed. In El Paso, Pops was also brand-new, starting a second life and getting remarried. And now JD thought about Danny. His father's surgery hadn't gone well. JD had texted yesterday, then again this morning. But all Danny's answers had been short. *Stroke. Still in the hospital. Nothing yet.* He thought about Amá and Tomás. About Isa and what she was doing at that exact moment.

Curtain glanced over at Rowe, so JD did the same. Dude was making his way over. "If he was talking about that dip-shit, then he's probably right. I got uncles like him. Have fun dealing with all that. I'm out." With that, Curtain turned and bolted, Peterson following right behind.

"Typical." Raines gently lifted his baby and sniffed her butt. "Well, I got other shit to deal with. I'm sorry too, man."

Raines disappeared into the party as JD tried to escape toward the back of the yard, but Rowe followed him. Clouds were gathering around the mountains, like they had all week. The sky turned gray, the air becoming crisp. Windy.

Rowe sidled up beside JD, stood shoulder to shoulder. "Your entourage abandoned you."

JD slid away from Rowe. He reeked of booze. "Did you come over here just to talk shit?" He was tired of this fool. Always loud. Always running his mouth. Getting his way.

There was a silence. The music had drifted inside the house, as did much of the party. Only a few pockets of partygoers were still outside. Rowe's family was gone too, and JD wondered if Rowe had stumbled away from them, or if it was the other way around.

Thunder boomed, the sound jolting JD.

"I don't think you can hold your own," Rowe finally said,

his words slow, wobbly. "And Raines, he talks too damn much. I'm gonna have my hands full with you two."

But JD could hold his own. He suddenly knew this. He'd made it through Basic, then tech school. Was already a decent wrench. He could run roads, trails. For miles and miles. Maybe he had joined the air force without thinking about it, but it *hadn't* been a mistake. A key had turned inside his head, finally unlocking the truth. He wasn't the flaky person everyone thought he was. And he for sure wasn't the loser he thought he'd been.

"Man, you should take your drunk ass inside. You're talking stupid."

It started to sprinkle.

Rowe looked confused as drops tapped against his face. "You can't talk to me like that. I'm your fuckin' boss. That's what I told the chief when I met with him last week. I'm the one in charge. You just got here, and Raines is leaving. I'm the one who's been here. It's my crew. I should get to go. That's the truth."

The truth. JD was more than a little embarrassed that he hadn't recognized Rowe's bullshit sooner. Rowe was constantly accusing JD of not knowing his job, accusing Raines of being a quitter, but what he was actually doing was telling on himself. Not only was Rowe a total faker, but the man was a snitch. All his accusations were complete confessions.

JD and Raines were the ones with their hands full.

JD looked over the back wall of the yard, then to Rowe. "I gotta go." JD hopped over the six-foot wall in one smooth jump, landing softly on the ground. He looked over to the mountain. Rowe was saying something, but JD ignored him, concentrating on the shrill, faraway yips of a coyote, its lone, mournful barks. In the distance he saw a figure cut across the brush, its slinky body maneuvering quickly before stopping abruptly. The coyote's eyes were bright, almost like stars burning on the mountainside, as it turned and faced JD. JD found himself holding his breath as he locked eyes with the animal, not breathing until it turned and sprinted into the darkness. He checked his watch.

He had one thing he needed to do before deploying.

There was time.

It rained. Hard. Outside of Deming, JD hammered down on the gas. The road was empty, except for the occasional slow-moving herd of semitrucks. He was past the halfway point to El Paso, just under an hour from Las Cruces. At night, New Mexico could pass for the surface of the moon, with long views of flat dark nothing with even darker mountain ranges in the distance. Hard pockets of wind swirled, whipping dirt and small pieces of loose rock. JD thought of pulling over. Of going back. But going back had been his original mistake.

Lightning ripped across the sky, everything bright but only for a flash. On the other side of the highway, cows were huddled underneath a mesquite tree, and a windmill's blades spun wildly.

JD had texted his old man, congratulating him on the wedding—even if he wasn't all that happy about it. He called Amá, promised he would call again before deploying. He'd been texting back and forth with Isa all week. Them joking and flirting. Just the idea of seeing her again made JD grin like an idiot.

Still nothing from Danny.

Last year the plan had been to drive Juan to the heart of Texas to meet his father. But they'd never made it. Instead, they'd ended up exactly where most of his, Juan's, and Danny's stories began. In Central. At the apartment. At Juan's.

CHAPTER SEVENTEEN
GOODBYE

The outside of the heart was a candy-apple red, a bright outline that encased the inner, exposed gear work. Danny wanted all the gears inside the heart to be red too. Only different shades. He'd mixed his own candy red, which he'd made with a base and some bright orange, adding a touch of gray. He then carefully painted the outside sprockets, his brushstrokes neat and precise, leaving each tooth perfectly mated with another. The next series of gears would be painted just a shade darker, Danny ready to add some sky blue to the mix. He would continue on this way, mixing and then painting, each row of gears becoming deep shades of crimson until he reached the center gear. The one about to break.

Roxanne was watching him, sitting, on the scaffolding that was now off to the side of the yard, legs dangling. The sun burned baldly in the sky above, directing a sheet of warm light onto them. Not a cloud to be seen. It had rained hard the night before, Danny's trays and plastic containers, left neatly beside the back wall of the property, were now filled with dirty pools of water at the bottoms. He had anxiously examined the rest of the mural before starting this morning, making sure none of his previous work had washed away. Luckily, the paint had already absorbed into the wall and was now bone dry. Or maybe it was more than luck. God knew Danny needed something good to happen. For someone, or something, to be watching over him now.

The Sarge was gone.

He'd died in the middle of the night. Danny and Má had been in the waiting room, both needing a break from the ISO room, when Dr. Rivera came inside. The doctor looked just as worn down as they did, her eyes with dark circles like bruises underneath them, the color drained from her face. Danny could tell by her expression—the utterly defeated look—that his father was dead.

The Sarge's body was still in the isolation room. All the machines, the tubes and wires that had been poking through his chest, were gone. The room cleared out. Except for him. A clean, crisp white blanket had been placed over him, pulled chest high and neatly tucked around and into the corners of the bed. The Sarge's arms were exposed and resting at his sides.

Má stood by the Sarge. She had gone in first, alone.

His face was swollen but clean, looked like his father. Like the soldier Danny had always known. Má was holding his hand, looking intently at him. The Sarge's hands still felt rough, warm as Danny entered the room and grabbed his other one. Tears streamed down Má's face, her breathing short. Jagged. Danny wanted his own tears to come. He squeezed his eyes shut, tensed his entire body. He could feel himself gripping his father's hand as he tried summoning them. *Nothing*. He'd felt this same way when Juan died. A growing void inching across his body, starting in his belly and then his chest. Moving across his thoughts until they blanked too.

With morning only a few hours away, Dr. Rivera came and gently ushered them from the room. She suggested someone drive Danny home. That he should rest—that they all needed to. But Má needed to stay at the hospital for a little while longer, her needing to sign some forms. Tío Fernando and Tía Carmen agreed to stay behind with Má. Roxanne would take Danny home.

As soon as the sun peeked out hours later, Roxanne didn't argue about going back to Juan's apartment, volunteering to drive, seeming to get that Danny needed to do this—to do *something*. That he was just like his father.

It had been only a week since Danny'd started the job. One week changed so much. Now Juan's old backyard was completely transformed. The weeds were all gone. The trash picked up.

And, of course, there was the mural itself. The Lotería tabla Danny had envisioned was almost complete. El Pescado and El Venado were on the first floor, El Soldado in between them. Not sure how he managed it, but Tata's face looked exactly like it had in the portrait hanging in the Sarge's office, his face tight, eyes squinting, his mouth almost a straight line. Danny had always thought Tata—and the Sarge—looked hard in their army photos, like the soldiers they were. Both of them ready to fight. But now Danny wondered if Tata didn't look more worried than brave.

La Muerte and El Borracho, La Dama, were above them on the second floor. La Muerte looked sinister, the mirrored sunglasses matching the gleam of his scythe's blade and badge. Death's sickly yellow bones poking grotesquely from underneath the cold blue policeman's uniform.

Danny paused now at El Borracho's—at JD's—face. He'd captured him almost exactly, using confident brushstrokes that had gotten the eyes near perfect. El Borracho's brown eyes were unfocused and haunted, a distant light reflecting in them. La Dama could've been an old photo of Fabi from her bartending days, a defiant smirk on her face and tray of beers balanced on her upturned hand. All Danny had left to complete the mural was to finish the heart, the final card between the two rows, right in the middle of the building. He was down to the final gear. The one about to break and shatter everything.

"Holy shit," a voice called out from behind him. "I look like a fucking junkie." JD lumbered toward Danny and Roxanne from the alley. Like Danny, he looked like he'd been up all night, his face weary and exhausted. He wore an air force T-shirt and jeans.

"Actually, you look like a fucking narc," Danny said, turning toward JD.

JD waved at Roxanne, who jumped off the scaffolding. "I got rained on. I had this shirt in my car. And I was driving all night. Give me a break."

"My dad died last night," Danny said.

"I had a bad feeling," JD said, the news still stopping him cold. "I just knew something was wrong, so I drove." He and Danny stared at each other, neither sure what to say. Finally, JD moved the rest of the way toward Danny and pulled him into a hug, an awkward squeeze. "I'm sorry."

"Thanks," Danny said blankly, the empty feeling in his body growing more hollow.

"It's good to see you," Roxanne said, trying to ease a growing tension. "As you can see, we finished."

"Sorry, I'm a piece-of-shit friend," JD said, wiping at the tears now pooling in his eyes.

"It's okay," Danny said. "We didn't need you."

"I only helped with the weeds and trash," Roxanne said. "Danny did all the painting."

"It looks good," JD said, scanning the wall. "Let's see. You got a death cop. Drunk me. Fabi. A soldier. A fish. A deer. And a big mechanical heart. I like it."

"They're Lotería cards. They sorta tell the story about what happened. What's happening."

JD looked over the wall, card by card. "I recognize the cards. You'll have to run me through all the story stuff, though I think I get some of it." His eyes returned to the version of him slumped by a busted window. A half-drunk 40 in his hand. "Man, I look like total hell."

"It's a beautiful memorial," Roxanne said.

"Juan would've liked it," JD added slowly, looking, and looking again. "I guess I was wrong. About leaving it the way it was."

"*I* wouldn't call it a memorial," Danny said, remembering

the giant murals painted on the highway columns at Lincoln Park, how those paintings were underneath the roads above, cars always coming and going. "This isn't our neighborhood anymore. You're gone. I'm gone . . . Juan's gone. A memorial is for remembering dead people. This mural is a story. It's a love letter. It's for remembering the way things used to be without forgetting how things are or can be."

JD moved away from Danny and Roxanne, walking down the middle of the pathway Danny had made, the colorful rocks set firm in the ground, not a wobble. Taking a close look at El Pescado and El Venado. At El Soldado.

Danny grabbed his palette and brush. "How did you end up back here? You didn't know we'd be here."

"You should paint a little coyote on the mountain right there," JD said, pointing at the mountains in the background of El Soldado. He shrugged and then nodded at his likeness. "I also needed to apologize to that kid right there, the one I ditched here the night Juan died. Who I blamed for Juan dying." He jammed his hands into his pockets, looked apologetically at Danny, his eyes glassy. "And I am sorry about your dad. You gotta know that I am."

"I do." And he did. Danny felt tears beginning to build and swirled his brush in the deep red paint, the color dark and earthy. He filled in the final gear, stopping the heart.

JUAN LAST CHANCE

ACT THREE

"WAR"

EXT. BUNKER/AIRPORT RUNWAY-NIGHT

JD and Hermosillo sit on the Taj Mahal of bunkers, a mountain of olive drab sandbags lining concrete barriers. They are smoking cigarettes and watching as A10s rumble down the runway.

It is NOISY as the jets take flight. One after the other.

HERMOSILLO
Good job helping with that hydraulic leak tonight. And changing the brakes.

JD
I was bored.

HERMOSILLO
(Laughing)
Sanchez, you're so full of shit. You got lifer written all over you.

Another jet RUMBLES down the runway behind them, gets airborne.

JD
I'm doing my four and bouncing, going to school right after.

HERMOSILLO
Doubt it.

A SIREN begins to wail. Neither JD nor Hermosillo looks particularly excited. They both continue to smoke, making no move to shelter in the bunker they are sitting on.

JD

(Stares at Hermosillo)

You don't know me.

HERMOSILLO

I don't know the sad little story that got you here. But I know how it goes from here.

The siren continues to wail. The intensity INCREASES. JD studies Hermosillo, trying to figure out if he's full of shit or not. JD pulls another cigarette out of his pack and lights it with the one he is smoking.

JD

Whatever.

HERMOSILLO

When your first enlistment is up, you'll have no place to go. And no way are you going back home. You ain't the type that goes backward. In four years, you'll have met some girl. Maybe be married. Probably have a kid. What are you *really* gonna do?

JD flicks his old cigarette butt onto the ground. It burns itself out, the glowing orange ember slowly turning black.

JD

Is that what happened to you?

HERMOSILLO
Happens to all the lifers.

FLASHBACK TO THAT MORNING

INT. JD'S TENT/TENT CITY-DAY

JD sits on his bunk, dressed in a T-shirt and basketball shorts. On his bed is his copy of *The People of Paper*, splayed open, and a spiral notebook filled with handwritten notes: *How Did We Get Here?* scrawled across the top.

His bed is by the tent's opening. Beams of light cut through the thick vinyl flap door. JD stares into the screen of his phone, swipes at it.

There are two rows of bunks running down each side of the tent, aluminum frames with thin mattresses. Some have mounds of dirty clothes piled on them, and others are neatly made. The grossest are littered with half-eaten bags of chips and candy wrappers.

Fourteen beds for fourteen dudes.
The tent appears empty, until JD grabs his notebook and walks down the center, toward the back, where two metal folding chairs have been set up facing each other.

PETERSON, CURTAIN, and RAINES are sitting on a bunk. ROWE is standing beside them with his arms crossed. Across from them is LUÍS, locking his smartphone into a tripod. They watch as JD approaches.

ROWE
So Petey says this is some kind

of movie. They all agreed to be
in it.

JD
Yup. A documentary. I want to
interview the guys a bunch of
times while we're here.

JD turns to the guys.

JD
You guys still down for that?

Everyone nods in agreement. Rowe glares at them, then at JD.

RAINES
I thought you wanted to do like
Hollywood movie type stuff.

JD
I started making a doc last year,
and I wanna finish that first.
But I'm gonna do that after. Bet.

JD sets his phone into another tripod opposite Luís. He looks into the screen and then moves to other camera, adjusts it.

JD
(To Luís)
I want to get the background of
the tent too, not just big dumb
face shots.

LUÍS
Got it.

Rowe walks over to the chairs, taps one with his foot.

ROWE

No one asked me to be in this.

JD

Is that why you're here? You wanna be in the movie?

ROWE

I just gotta make sure you're not doing anything fucked up. I'm the boss, ya know?

JD

I didn't think you'd give a shit. This is also to help me get into film school. I know how you are about that.

ROWE

I don't. You wannabe college boys always think you're better than us regular guys. Always trying to prove it.

JD

(An idea forming)

Why don't you go first? Say what you gotta say. Tell me all about regular guys.

JD takes a seat and offers the other folding chair to Rowe, who eyeballs JD for a beat before slowly accepting. He uncomfortably shifts in his seat.

JD nods at Luís, who starts both cameras, then gives JD a thumbs-up.

JD
(Pauses)
I was gonna have everyone start with what life was like back home before joining. So you could talk to me about Florida or whatever, about growing up, or you could say whatever else you wanted.

JD looks over at Luís, who gives a second thumbs-up as he pokes the screen of the camera phone. He walks over to the other camera and again hits record.

Rowe and JD stare hard at each other, neither saying a word.

JD
Okay. Here we go. Sergeant Rowe. Action.

BACK TO THE SCENE

EXT. BUNKER-CONTINUOUS

JD and Hermosillo watch as the groups of airman in the distance scramble from the flight line and run toward them. JD smooshes his cigarette into a sandbag and slides off the bunker.

JD
Well, that lifer shit ain't happening to me. I'm going to film school, one way or another.

HERMOSILLO

All I'm saying, Sanchez, is that you're really good at this. The guys already follow you. You could go as far as you want. You could be a chief.

JD and Hermosillo crawl inside the bunker.

CUT TO:

INT. BUNKER-CONTINUOUS

JD and Hermosillo are holding glow sticks, the dull green glow lighting their faces as they look out the bunker's opening. The siren is still WAILING. The rest of the airmen are upon them.

JD

I'm not really the be-in-charge type. Man, you really don't know me.

HERMOSILLO

I guess not. But I hope you're good at movies, then. Trading the family cow for magic beans don't always work out, Jack.

The bunker begins to fill with JD and Hermosillo's fellow airmen, with sounds of nervous talking, murmuring. Hermosillo and JD slide over to make room.

JD looks at his hands under the green glow as he is squished between Hermosillo and another airman. They are covered with black grease, gunk embedded underneath his fingernails. The bunker is now packed.

There is the faraway sound of an EXPLOSION, and inside, the bunker goes deathly silent. Everyone waiting for what happens next as muffled sirens continue to WAIL.

27

EL CORAZÓN

"No me extrañes corazón, que regreso en el camión"

You stand at the podium, at the altar, of Our Lady of Guadalupe. The church you used to go to when you were a kid, before you moved to the new house. The one the Sarge went to before he tried a new church, then no church at all. Má asked you if you would do one of the readings. That it would mean a lot. As you read, you're not sure what anything means.

The surgery that was supposed to save your father's life didn't. He died hours later from a stroke. His heart fixed but that not good enough. The doctor explained everything to you and Má while standing in the isolation room, in the empty space where the Sarge, his hospital bed, had just been.

She is sorry for your loss.

A priest stands next to you as you now read from the book of the Prophet Daniel. He doesn't know you, but he places his hand on your shoulder. He smiles, his face big and warm. You want to sock him in his dumb mouth, but instead you continue reading.

Many of those who sleep in the dust of the earth shall awake.

The Sarge is going to be buried at Fort Bliss National Cemetery, same place as his father. At the funeral home, you spoke on the phone with a man from the cemetery. He asked you about your father's service. What you wanted on his headstone. You answered:

DANIEL VILLANUEVA.

MSG.

US ARMY.

SOUTHERN WATCH.

ENDURING FREEDOM.

IRAQI FREEDOM.

Do you wanna just put Global War on Terrorism instead? the man had asked. *It'll be cheaper.*

You are finally crying, trying to breathe and read at the same time. You make eye contact with Roxanne. She nods at you. A gesture that means everything is okay, to go ahead and cry all you want. You pull out your father's memorial card from the breast pocket of your jacket. You want to look at him just one more time. Of course the Sarge is in uniform. His face blank, steely.

You keep reading.

Some shall live forever, others shall be an everlasting horror and disgrace.

But the wise shall shine brightly like the splendor of the firmament.

The pews are packed. Má is in the front, sitting beside Tío Fernando and Tía Carmen. At least three rows of other tíos and tías, primos you rarely see, behind them. There are soldiers filling the rest of the church. Their faces looking right at the casket just below the altar, below you. An American flag is perfectly draped, fifty perfect white stars against the deepest blue shrouding the Sarge's coffin.

You gently rub the image of your father between your fingers. The oils from them slightly smearing his image. You're still crying.

The tears come and come.

The priest squeezes your shoulder, a compassionate gesture but also a signal that you can't stop reading now.

And you won't.

You finished all the murals, but there are now more to do. Pablo has sent work your way. A daycare wanting cartoon animals, something soft and cuddly. A barbershop wanting giant clippers and scissors. You are taking Roxanne's place at the bakery and a semester—maybe more—off from school.

You will never be a soldier. You are what comes after. Exactly how the Sarge wanted it to be.

You take a deep breath and finish strong.

And those who lead the many to justice shall be like the stars forever.

37

EL MUNDO

"Este mundo es una bola, y nosotros un bolón"

You sit in the recovery room, holding your baby to your chest. He is small, warm, swaddled in a white towel. His tiny hand presses against his cheek, balled into a tight fist. His eyes are wide open, him silently looking to you.

You are twenty-three years old.

A man.

Married and in love.

You are the same age your father was when he split from the army. Him wanting his shot at civilian life. At the American Dream.

But you are not your father, not going to lose sleep chasing dreams for yourself. You have your own son now.

You reenlisted. Will gladly take two hots and a cot. The steady paycheck that always comes.

Sandra is still in surgery, the final part of the C-section. You rock your new son back and forth. Your first attempt at soothing him. At making him feel safe.

Right now you and your son are the only two people in the room, maybe the universe. You think of the stars you've always loved and how what makes them is now inside your boy. Not just oxygen and carbon and hydrogen but also mystery. His eyes already gleaming with it.

"I'll never let you down," you lie, even though you mean it more than anything you've ever thought or said. "Never."

Through the window you see clouds stretched against the denim-blue sky, pulling apart like bright white cotton.

Daniel Villanueva II.

Sandra was the one who wanted to give him your name. *It's an inheritance*, she explained.

A nurse wheels Sandra into the recovery room. She looks beautiful, her eyes tired but bright. Stars of their own.

"Skin to skin," the nurse says. "It's time for mama and baby to bond."

You hand your brand-new world to Sandra, who cradles him before gently unwrapping him, the nurse helping Sandra place the baby's bare body against her chest. You are already losing him. Outside, the sun hides behind the thinning clouds, soft light filling the room.

A feeling of possibility, a seed long dormant inside your chest, is suddenly sprouting.

The moment is perfect.

Your boy is perfect.

You start to cry.

Your heart, your life, is full.